DOUBLE PLAY

WHEN THE GAME OF DECEIT CAN NEVER BE UNBROKEN

K. REDD

First paperback edition August 2022
Published by Dream Fierce Publishing, LLC

Book design by Nick Castle

ISBN 979-8-9861449-1-7 (paperback)
ISBN 979-8-9861449-0-0 (ebook)

Library of Congress Control Number: 2022910812

Contents

Acknowledgments

I would like to thank my parents for all of the love and support they have provided throughout my lifetime. I would also like to thank other members of my family and friends who have supported me in the publishing of my book. I would like to show my gratitude to Daniel Northington for reviewing early copies of my manuscript and providing guidance. I would also like to thank my editors at Kevin Anderson and Associates and Publishing Life Services and beta readers who helped strengthen my book in every way.

Prologue

Sometimes, it is possible to be too conspicuous. People often say everyone is connected to everyone else in the world within six degrees of separation. As a successful luxury and exotic car salesman who drove a flashy car, Ryan Wright was connected to many people—good and bad. He was the salesman of choice for celebrities and high-powered politicians and had a certain amount of flashiness that stood out. Even people who did not know Ryan noticed him as he drove down the street.

TOMMIE

Tommie Parker loved everything about cars. In fact, he loved cars so much, he decided to become a mechanic. He fantasized about owning a large collection of luxury and exotic cars one day. However, his life as a mechanic was short-lived as he spent life in and out of prison for petty theft and armed robbery. Frequently accused but seldom convicted, Tommie, nevertheless, had a lot of luck on his side.

Tommie first noticed Ryan's car driving down the highway one day after Tommie's cousin picked him up from his latest stint in jail. He made his cousin follow the car for miles, leading them to the luxury and exotic car dealership where Ryan worked. Sitting parked outside the gates of the dealership, Tommie told his cousin all about several cars at the dealership. He described everything about their engines, safety features, and options until his cousin became annoyed and drove away.

One day, Tommie scheduled an appointment to meet with Ryan about buying a car. He could not afford any of the cars at the dealership, but he wanted to get a closer look at them and take one for a test drive. On the day of the appointment, Tommie put on his best suit and had his brother drive him to the dealership. As Tommie entered the dealership, he noticed a slight tear in his suit jacket. He immediately felt as if everyone was staring at him and thinking that he did not belong there. The receptionist greeted Tommie and paged Ryan.

Ryan came out and shook Tommie's hand. "Hello,

Mr. Parker. Can you tell me what type of car you're looking for?"

"Well, everything looks great."

"Is there a specific make and model you want? Or are you looking for specific features?"

Tommie tugged at his suit jacket and folded his arm over the tear. "Well, I love cars. I like every make and every model. I really want to test-drive all of them to see which one I like best. It doesn't matter what I test first." Tommie appeared oddly giddy, unlike Ryan's usual customers.

"Okay, in order for you to test-drive a car, I need to make a copy of your driver's license and car insurance."

"Oh, I don't have those with me."

"That's not a problem. I can schedule an appointment for you to test-drive a car on another day. Meanwhile, I can show you—"

"Please, can I just test-drive one today? I don't need to take it out of the parking lot. I can just drive around the lot."

"I'm sorry, sir. That's not the way we do things here." Ryan signaled for the security guard to keep an eye on him.

Tommie became agitated. "You discriminating against me 'cause of the way I look? You don't think I look rich enough to have a car like this?" Tommie paced, scrunched his face, and pointed at Ryan. His voice increased in intensity. "I'm gonna report you to the news and my lawyer, and you'll be sorry you ever treated me like this."

The security guard quickly approached Tommie. "Sir, you need to leave now."

"You ain't gonna stop me. I will get a car." Tommie yelled as the security guard escorted him out of the dealership.

When the security guard returned, he approached Ryan. "Man, what was that about? You makin' enemies like that?"

Ryan shrugged his right shoulder. "I have no idea what was going on with him. That was weird. Must be on drugs or something."

MARCO

Marco Kameron was always a frugal man who worked hard and played by the rules. Although he grew up poor, he was determined to make sure that his future children did not have to experience the hardships he experienced. After college, Marco found a job at a small investment banking firm and made sure he stayed away from his childhood peers who had chosen a life of crime. He married a beautiful, funny, and intelligent woman named Veronica, and, in many ways, he had the perfect life and was happy.

Marco first met Ryan Wright when he decided to

surprise his wife with a luxury car after he caught her ogling one at a local shopping mall. He could not afford a new luxury car, but he knew that many new car dealerships also sold used cars. His wife, Veronica, deserved to be spoiled. She endured a difficult pregnancy along with complications during the birth of their son. In the months following his birth, Veronica showed what a wonderful mother she was in addition to being a wonderful wife. On the day of the surprise, Marco and his wife met with Ryan, who sold them a used, candy red Maserati.

Three days later, while Marco was on his way home from work, he saw something that changed his life forever. Two blocks from his home, the street was completely blocked off with yellow crime scene tape. As Marco began to reverse his car, he looked up and noticed that a red Maserati was parked askew on the other side of the tape. Marco felt dizzy and faint as he exited his car and darted toward the Maserati.

"Stop right there!" An officer stepped in front of Marco and grabbed him firmly. "You can't cross an active crime scene."

"Get off me!" Marco roared, shaking himself free. He edged closer to the Maserati and noticed several bullet holes in the car's doors and windows. Shattered glass was strewn on the ground near the car. A splatter of scarlet stained the driver's side window. Marco could see his wife's body hunched over the steering wheel. His legs went numb as he crumpled onto the gravel. "No. No, no, no..."

One of the officers standing near the Maserati approached Marco. "Excuse me, sir?"

"My wife. That's my wife," Marco said as tears streamed down his cheeks. "And...where's my son?"

"I'm so sorry. There was a baby in the backseat. He was also killed."

After endless questioning by investigators, Marco was finally allowed to go home. He felt his mind wandering to the bloodstained car window all night. Why would someone want to murder his wife? An overwhelming clutch of anguish sat in his stomach and the shock paralyzed him. The guilt he felt from failing to protect his wife and child ate at his soul. He barely ate or slept, and his humanity dissolved further with each passing day.

Weeks passed, and the police still had no clues about who killed Marco's wife and son. Marco was determined to make everyone and anyone who played a role in what happened pay. He became obsessed with avenging the deaths of his wife and son and feverishly made a list of everyone who had any contact with his wife shortly before her death. His desire for vengeance fueled his anger. Everyone responsible for his wife's death had to die.

Every day, Marco selected at least two people on his twenty-page list to stalk. He spent hours researching them online before driving to their homes and following them throughout the day. As he drove, his hands ached from having punched walls, tables, and everything within his sight the prior evening. When Marco finally located his target, he clenched his jaw in anger and cried until tears no longer flowed as he scribbled detailed notes about the target onto his tattered notepad.

Although Marco had stayed away from a life of crime, he knew how to reach many of his childhood acquaintances who had chosen the criminal career path. His body trembled as he spent most of the night contacting everyone who could help with his plans. His daily routine left about two hours for sleep, which usually only happened when he passed out onto the floor somewhere.

DREW

Drew Ronstone purchased numerous luxury cars from Ryan Wright's co-worker, Kale Jones. Kale had no idea what Drew did for a living or where his money came from; he only knew that Drew was a regular customer who paid cash and helped him to compete with Ryan's sales. Sometimes, Kale bought used cars from Drew to sell at the dealership. The cars were always customized with unique colors, tinted windows, and custom tires and rims. Kale met with Drew at his garage five times per year. One day, Kale called in sick and asked Ryan if he could meet with his longtime client instead.

The meeting was to take place at Drew's business after hours; Kale assured Ryan that Drew was a good guy. Ryan was hesitant to meet with a customer he did not know personally, especially late in the evening. However, Kale assured Ryan there were no safety issues and promised to let him keep all commissions from the sale.

As Ryan walked toward Drew's massive, multi-car garage, he quickly glanced up at the night sky, focusing on the stars for a few seconds. He always got a little nervous entering late-night meetings, so he looked for ways to calm his mind.

When Ryan reached the garage, he typed the passcode provided by Kale and entered the garage as soon as the door unlocked. There were eight men standing around a red Maserati. A short, stout man approached Ryan.

"Ah, you must be Ryan. Kale told me all about you." Drew approached Ryan and shook his hand.

"Nice car. Are you buying or selling?" Ryan circled the Maserati, examining the exterior.

"Come to my office and show me what you got. I'll have somethin' ready for you or Kale to pick up tomorrow."

Ryan followed Drew to his office and pulled out photos and descriptions of available cars for sale. Drew picked out one vehicle and pulled a stack of cash out of his office safe and handed it to Ryan. Ryan quickly flipped through the bills.

Drew walked over to his office door and opened it. "It's all there plus a little extra for your time."

Ryan stuffed the cash into his briefcase. "How would you like the receipt?"

"We work out of trust. You trust I gave you enough money. I trust you will give me what I ordered."

Two days after Ryan left, police surrounded Drew's garage. Shots were exchanged, but the police were able to capture and arrest Drew along with two of his workers. While in prison awaiting his arraignment, Drew called his cousin Tony.

Tony answered in a husky tone as he coughed. "Hey, Drew, what's up?"

"Did you hear about what happened to me?"

"Yeah, the whole family's talkin' about it. Do you know who caused it?" Tony continued to cough.

"I don't know for sure, but Alex has been acting strange lately. Also, it happened a couple of days after I met with that other car dealer, Kale's guy." Drew looked around to see if any of the other prisoners were watching him. "I think his name was Ryan something. Oh yeah, Ryan Wright. It just seems like too much of a coincidence."

"I'll see what I can find out. You think that Ryan guy might have been working with the police?"

"That's what I'm thinking. I worked with Kale for years without so much as a peep from the police."

"I'm on it. And Alex?"

Drew glanced over at the guard standing nearby and lowered his voice. "One of my guys said he was under-cover, and he's been acting funny lately."

"Okay, I got you. I will take care of everything, and if you need anything else, just let me know."

"Your loyalty will be rewarded," Drew said before hanging up the phone.

One

After spending their entire lives switching places and getting away with it, Brian Wright and his identical twin brother had no idea their lives were going to change forever. Their workday began in a normal way. Every weekday, they spent early morning hours at a fitness center before working together at a California luxury and exotic car dealership where Brian was manager and Ryan was the top salesperson.

Like many days before, Ryan walked into Brian's office, tossed his keys onto Brian's desk, and scooped up the set of keys perched on the desk's corner near the edge. It was switch day, which meant trading cars, homes, and families for a day.

"Hey, don't crash my car!" Ryan said with a sly smile

as he slid Brian's keys into his pocket. His green eyes sparkled as he shot Brian a mischievous look.

Brian abruptly pivoted toward Ryan. "Yeah, yeah, yeah. When was the last time I crashed a car? You're the reckless one. Make sure you leave everything as YOU found it."

"Hmm... I seem to remember that one time, ten or fifteen years ago. A totaled car and a speeding ticket with your name written all over it." Ryan turned and walked out of the office.

Brian jumped out of his seat and leaned forward, plopping his fists onto his desk. "Man, don't even play! You were the one in the accident, and you're the one who was speeding!"

Ryan rushed back into Brian's office and stood in the doorway. "Well, as far as everyone else knows, it was all you." Ryan laughed. "And that's all that really matters."

"I'm gonna get you back for that one."

Sharon, the finance manager, stomped into the office, sliding in front of Ryan. As she entered, her foot-long curly red hair practically slapped Ryan in the face. "Hey, guys, is everything okay in here?" Sharon turned her head toward Ryan, pushed her overly long bangs out of her face, and squinted her eyes, peeking at his name tag. "Uh, Ryan?"

"The show's over. Bye, Sharon!"

"I'm just... Never mind. I just heard loud voices. Anyway, I'm so glad you guys wear name tags. I wouldn't be able to tell you apart without them." Sharon left the office, creating a small earthquake with every step.

Ryan grasped the door handle and pulled the door closed. "She has to mention the name tags every single day. Doesn't she know this is your office, so if she sees you sitting here, she should know who you are?"

"You know she just has to say something." Brian rotated in his chair and typed on his computer keyboard.

Ryan unfastened his name tag and placed it onto Brian's desk. "I'm just going to leave this here. I'm running late. What time are you getting out of here?"

"In a couple of hours. Where are you going?" Brian asked without glancing up from his computer.

"I just have an errand to run before heading home. Don't worry, I won't be too late." Ryan pulled his cell phone out of his pocket and peeked at it before quickly slipping it back into his pocket. "Okay, we'll talk later."

"You know we need to—"

"I know, I know." Ryan raised his arm above his head, waved his hand, and dashed out of Brian's office. *Blip, Blip.* A text arrived. Ryan reached in his pocket and slid out his phone.

It was from his wife, Amanda. *Don't forget, we have the counseling session this eve. Let me know if you need the address again. I will be on video.* Ryan sighed. He had forgotten all about the appointment with the marriage counselor. He replied, *I will be a little late. Feel free to start without me.* Ryan slid the phone back into his pocket. *Blip, Blip.* Ryan sighed as he glanced at his phone again. *WTF?* He decided to ignore his wife's last message and headed back to his desk.

It was the end of the day, and the sun was setting. Brian walked outside of the car dealership with keys dangling from his right hand and headed toward Ryan's carmine red Porsche 911. He approached the car and pulled the door handle. Suddenly, he saw his co-worker Kale jogging toward him flailing his noodle-like arms. Ryan chuckled. He wasn't sure if Kale was trying to get his attention or if he was doing a crazy dance.

"Hey, Ryan," said Kale, breathing heavily. "Don't get too comfortable at the top. You know you only got the most sales because I gave you that deal with Drew."

At first Brian was slightly confused, but then he realized that Kale thought he was Ryan. "Man, get out of here. You know I had more sales than you for the past year. I didn't need that Drew deal."

As Brian stepped into Ryan's Porsche, he danced with

giddiness. Not only did his dealership have the top quarterly sales in the nation, but there was something satisfyingly thrilling about driving at top speed while checking for state troopers perched along a curvy mountain highway. Brian slid his cell phone out of his pocket and dialed Ryan's number. Ryan answered.

"Hey, man, where you at?"

"I'm just leaving a meeting." Ryan's voice seemed somewhat muffled and was much lower than usual.

"Oh, okay. What time will you be home?"

"We'll talk later." Ryan quickly hung up the phone.

Brian wondered what was going on with Ryan. He usually never hung up without providing pertinent details about his plans for the day and saying goodbye. Before starting the car, Brian called his wife, Kira.

"Hey, I'm just leaving work. How was your day?"

"Pretty good, but it seemed as if most of my students ate a ton of sugar over the weekend. They were practically bouncing off the walls all day. Oh, before I forget, I think you may need to call someone about the sprinkler system. It didn't come on today. Or maybe you can check to see if you can figure out what's wrong. Also, can you pick up some butter from the store? I forgot that we ran out."

"Will do. Anything else?" Brian pressed the ignition button to start the car.

"No, not that I can think of. Oh, Jessica got an A on her book report."

"That's great! She's already doing book reports in the first grade?"

"Well, their definition of a book report is not the same as it is for older grades. It was only a few sentences. Of course, I helped her write it." Kira giggled.

"Well, I have some great news too. I'm getting a huge bonus from work. Sales were off the charts last month! A vacation is definitely in the works."

"Sounds good, but remember the school schedule."

"Maybe a quick weekend trip for now?"

"Yep, sounds like a plan. I'll see you when you get home."

"Okay, bye, babe." Brian ended the call and sent a quick text to Ryan about picking up some butter and calling someone about the sprinkler system.

Ryan responded with the letter *K*. Brian cranked up the music and pulled out of the parking space. Suddenly, he received a text from Ryan. *Alarm set off. Home searched. Nothing found.*

Brian was unsure about what Ryan meant in his text, but he wasn't too concerned. He was too busy basking in the glow of victory of having such a great day. Brian drove through the parking lot and headed out toward the highway while bobbing his head and shaking his shoulders to the music.

As Brian headed to Ryan's home for his switch life day, he thought about how he planned to spend his evening. Brian switched everything with his brother every two or three days. Although Brian loved spending time with his beautiful wife, Kira, he looked forward to spending some rest and relaxation time in Ryan's home. Ryan's wife, Amanda, was on a business trip with no plan to return until Sunday. Although Ryan's toddler would be home, the nanny always kept her busy and took care of her basic needs, so Brian usually just played with her before going to bed. His plans for the evening included playing with his niece, ordering food to be delivered, and spending time on the phone with Ryan rehashing the day's events and discussing plans for the following day. Oh, and let's not forget the massage chair. His favorite part of Ryan's home was the luxury massage chair. He spent hours relaxing and dozing in it.

Brian glanced in the rearview mirror and noticed a black car following closely behind him. As he exited the highway, it continued to follow him. Instead of immediately driving to Ryan's home, he drove around a nearby neighborhood. Eventually, the other car turned the corner and drove in the opposite direction.

Brian pulled up to the gate in front of Ryan's mansion. Ryan's home was far behind a black security gate. The home had a well-manicured yard designed with security in mind. There were many bushes and flowering trees blocking the home and driveway from public view. Some trees near the driveway had flowered, dropping scented petals along the path.

As Brian entered the code to open the gate, he noticed that the gate was already unlocked, so he drove up the driveway toward the house. While he slowly cruised up the long, curved driveway, something suddenly crashed through his rear windshield and struck the back of his seat. Brian brought the car to an abrupt stop and hopped out of the car.

"What in the world!" Brian exclaimed as he leaned into the car and examined the driver's seat. There was a silver metal item lodged into the headrest. It was a bullet. Panicked, Brian jumped back...suddenly, something hit him in the chest. He looked down and saw blood on his shirt. Staring at the blood, he felt faint and fell to the ground after blacking out. His cell phone fell out of his pocket and slid under the car.

A burly fellow wearing earbuds and talking to someone on his cell phone approached Brian. When he reached Brian, he rolled him over with his foot and bent over to look at him. Then he grabbed the back of Brian's head and slammed his forehead against the pavement. "I'm done here. Ready for pickup." After five minutes, a white cargo van with dark tinted windows sped up the driveway and parked behind Ryan's car. A slender man jumped out of the van and opened the trunk doors. The two men picked up Brian and carried him to the van, where they tossed him into the trunk before driving away.

Ryan was worried because he had been calling and texting Brian for over an hour. Brian always returned calls and replied to text messages promptly. Ryan decided to stop by his home to see if Brian was okay. When Ryan arrived at his home, he sped up the driveway. As the Porsche came into Ryan's view, relief quickly turned to worry when he noticed the car was parked with the door wide open. Something was wrong. Ryan stopped the car, hopped out, and sprinted toward the Porsche. Ryan noticed a puddle of what appeared to be blood on the cement. He quickly grabbed his cell phone and dialed Brian's number. Ryan heard Brian's ringtone. It seemed nearby, so he searched around and inside the Porsche. Finally, he located Brian's phone under the Porsche's trunk next to one of the tires. Ryan hesitated, but he knew what he had to do. He scooped up Brian's phone and used it to call the police.

After speaking with the police, Ryan powered off his cell phone and removed the battery before shoving it into his pant pocket. Then he used Brian's phone to call his nanny.

"Hello."

"Hello, Anne?"

"Oh, hi, Brian."

"Actually, this is... I mean, have you seen my brother today?"

"Um, no. Is something wrong?"

"Yeah, I couldn't reach him, so I stopped by and saw blood near his car parked in the driveway. I can't find him anywhere." Ryan looked around the yard in every direction as he walked toward the house.

"Oh, I've been busy getting Olivia ready for bed. I didn't hear him get home." As Anne spoke, Ryan heard his daughter Olivia whining in the background saying that she did not want to go to bed. "Excuse me. Olivia, go pick out a book for me to read before bed. I'm sorry about that. You said there was blood?"

"Yeah, I'm really worried. I don't know what could've happened. I called the police, so I'm going to wait here for them in the house. I have a key, so you don't need to let me in."

"Um, okay. Oh, there was a problem with the alarm today, but someone came to fix it." As Anne spoke, Ryan heard Olivia singing in the background. "Shh. Olivia, can you quiet down some? I'm on the phone."

"What was the problem?"

"Don't know. Um, when I came back from the park, the alarm was completely off. I know I set it before I left. I always do. Anyway, I called the alarm company to let them know I couldn't set the alarm, and they called back a couple of hours later and said they fixed it."

"Did you set the alarm after it was fixed?"

"Uh, no, I didn't have time to turn it on yet. I can set it now."

"That's okay. Leave it off for now. The police are on their way." Police sirens wailed in the background as two police cars pulled up into the driveway and parked behind Ryan's Porsche. "Anne, the police are here. I have to go. I'm sure they'll want to talk to you too." Ryan walked toward the police officers.

The police officers and detectives hopped out of their cars and walked around Ryan's Porsche. There were four police officers altogether. A few minutes later, additional officers arrived and began searching the entire property. One officer took pictures of the vehicle and the blood-stained cement. Another officer blocked off the driveway with caution tape. A police detective saw Ryan and approached him.

"Hi, I'm the one who called about my brother." Ryan

nervously shifted his weight from one leg to the other. He realized that it was too late for him to back out of pretending to be his brother. However, he was not comfortable providing false information to law enforcement.

"Do you know what happened here?" The detective yanked a small notepad and pencil out of his pocket.

Ryan studied the detective's face and noticed that he looked old enough to have a minimum of thirty years experience solving crimes. Good, he needed someone with experience who knew what he was doing. "No, sir. I came to check on my brother when he didn't respond to my messages and calls. That's when I came here and saw the blood." Ryan focused his eyes on the officers who had spread out around the yard as they examined the property.

"Well, that's certainly a lot of blood. Do you have any reason to believe that someone would have wanted to harm your brother?"

"No. Everyone loves my brother." Ryan turned away from the detective and glanced at the officers searching his yard. He pointed toward the outer perimeter of the yard. "Shouldn't someone be out there looking for him?"

"We'll get to that. When did you last see your brother? What's his name?"

Ryan's face glistened as sweat flowed from his pores. "Brian. I'm sorry. I'm just really upset." Ryan sighed as his fingers trembled. "My brother's name is Ryan. Ryan Wright. My name is Brian. Same last name."

"Okay, when did you last see your brother?"

"At work. I work with him and see him every day at the gym. We talk a lot. We're identical twins, so we are a lot alike, and we know most of the same people." Ryan took a deep breath as he realized he was rambling. "I left... I mean, he left work a little early. He said something about a meeting."

"Do you know who he was meeting?"

Ryan shrugged his right shoulder. "I assumed he was meeting with a customer."

"Does he keep a calendar at the office with his appointments?"

"Yeah, there is a shared online calendar, but I didn't see anything on it for today. Sometimes, he'll schedule a meeting at the last minute without adding it to the calendar."

"Did he mention where the meeting was being held?"

Ryan sighed. "No."

"And you said you're twins. Do you look alike?"

"Yes. We're identical. We look exactly alike."

"Well, even with identical twins, there are slight differences. How do people tell you apart?"

"They can't tell us apart. At work, we wear name tags. That's how they know."

The detective stared at Ryan suspiciously. "Well, we will continue our investigation to determine exactly what happened here. At this point, we don't even know if that's your brother's blood or if he is actually missing, but we will add his information to the database. Meanwhile, here's my card. Contact me immediately if you hear from him or if you have additional information that may be useful." The detective pulled out his wallet, grabbed a business card, and handed the card to Ryan.

"Oh, by the way, if you need to take a DNA sample to compare to the blood, you can use mine to see if that's my brother's blood. Since we're identical, we have the same DNA. Also, the nanny, Anne, is in the home. She might be able to provide some information."

"Okay, I will let CSI know about the DNA, and I will speak with the nanny. Is your brother married?"

"Yes, but his wife is away on a business trip. I can give you her phone number." Ryan gave the officer his wife's phone number and hopped into Brian's Lincoln Aviator. He sat in a daze as the detective walked up to the house and rang the doorbell. After several minutes, Anne flung the door partially open and stood in the doorway peeking out.

"Hey. Um, can I help you?"

"Hello, I'm Detective Grimes. Are you the nanny?"

"Um, yeah. I'm Anne." A gust of wind struck Anne's

head, shoving her light brown, shoulder-length hair across her face. She swept it away with her hand. The landscape lighting suddenly illuminated the yard as the sky darkened.

"I have some questions about your employer, Ryan Wright. When was the last time you saw him?" Detective Grimes glanced down at his notepad and held his pen poised over it ready to write.

"Yesterday evening, before I put Olivia to bed."

"Do you usually see him in the morning?"

"Uh, no. He goes to the gym every morning. I think he leaves about four or five o'clock, before I wake up."

"How long have you worked for the Wrights?"

"Um, three years. Since Olivia was a few months old."

"I see. Did you see anything or hear any unusual sounds outside today?"

"No." Anne turned toward Olivia, who was spinning around near the door. "Uh, can you excuse me? I just want to turn on a movie for her."

"Go ahead." The detective followed Anne and watched as she flipped through the television channels until Charlie Brown appeared on the screen. "So, were you here at the house all day?"

"No. Um, I was gone most of the day. I took Olivia to the playground for a while, and then I went grocery shopping. Oh, I also met a friend for lunch after the playground."

"How long were you gone?"

"Um, about four, five hours. I'm not sure. I left around ten o'clock in the morning and came home about four."

"To your knowledge, is there any reason someone would want to harm Mr. Wright?"

"Um, no. Not that I can think of. Brian mentioned something about blood. Is Mr. Wright okay?"

"That's what we're trying to find out. I want you to come down to the station tomorrow so we can take a more detailed statement. Here's my card. It has my direct number on it. Meanwhile, if you think of any additional information tonight that might be useful, call me right away." Several officers walked up to the front door. "Do you mind if these officers inspect the premises?"

Anne slowly shook her head. "Oh, wait. Maybe I should check with Mrs. Wright." Anne removed her cell phone from her pant pocket and dialed Mrs. Wright. After briefly explaining everything, Anne stepped aside so the police could enter.

After the detective and officers left the home, Anne picked up Olivia, who had fallen asleep on the living room sofa, and carried her upstairs to bed.

Meanwhile, Ryan sat in Brian's Aviator pondering the day's events. He leaned against the steering wheel and folded his arms over his head. What would he do without

Brian? He'd never known life without Brian, and he never imagined his life would exist without him. Even when they were apart, they were together as the thread that wove their lives together became tighter and tighter with each passing day. Did he do something to cause Brian's disappearance? Was Brian attacked due to mistaken identity because the attackers believed they were attacking him?

After the day his father died, this was Ryan's worse day ever. Not only was his brother missing and possibly dead, but the marriage counseling session with his wife, who called in instead of showing up in person, had not ended well. Which country was she in this time? He couldn't remember. Her 70 percent work travel schedule seemed more like 100 percent during the past year, and he wasn't sure the marriage could survive. Ryan had planned to tell Brian all about the counseling session, but he didn't get a chance. To make matters worse, he didn't know if he could tell anyone his true identity, especially after lying to the police.

Tap, tap, tap. Ryan lifted his head and looked up. An officer was tapping on the car window. Ryan rolled down the window as the officer peered inside.

"You can leave now," the officer said, waving Ryan away.

Ryan was surprised because he assumed he could leave whenever he wanted anyway. He started up Brian's car and picked up his brother's phone, cradling it in his hand. Should he call Amanda? Could he trust her to keep his secret until they found his brother? She was mad and might use any excuse to belittle him during their counseling sessions. Perhaps this was not the right time, Ryan thought. Later. He planned to tell her later. As he drove down the driveway, Anne peeked out of an upstairs window. Her phone rang.

"Hey, the police just left," Anne said cautiously. "Don't worry, they don't know anything." After ending the call, Anne closed the blinds and went to bed.

Two

TWENTY-FIVE YEARS EARLIER

Brian and Ryan were in their bedroom getting dressed for school. Their bedroom was small and contained a bunk bed and two small desks with chairs. Their mother, Margaret, stormed into the room.

"Brian, what is this?" she said, waving a piece of paper in the air.

"Huh?" Brian said as he buttoned his shirt.

"Don't huh me. What is this? A C in math? That is unacceptable. You know what I told you about the importance of doing your homework and studying."

Brian lowered his eyes toward the floor.

"Boy, look at me when I'm talking to you. Why didn't you tell me you were having trouble?"

Brian slowly raised his tear-filled eyes. "I don't know. I thought it would be higher."

Ryan jumped up after tying his shoes. "Mom, I'll help him with math. I got an A. He'll do better next time. I'll help him do better."

"Okay, well, I better see some higher grades or no birthday at the trampoline park for either of you." Margaret seemed satisfied that Brian would improve his math grade with Ryan's help. She left the room after giving each boy a good-night hug and kiss.

Brian walked closer to Ryan. "How are you gonna help me with math?"

Ryan shrugged his right shoulder. "I'll figure something out." After Ryan finished getting dressed, he turned toward Brian. "Hey, let me take your next math test."

"Huh?"

"Let me take your math test. They can't tell us apart. I'll take your test and help you get an A. We'll switch classes."

"What if we get caught?"

"Look in the mirror." Ryan pointed toward the full-length mirror leaning against the wall as he put his arm around Brian's shoulder. "How are they gonna know?"

"I don't know." Brian stared into the mirror for several minutes. "Okay, maybe one time."

Dozens of children were outside enjoying recess at a large inner-city school. Brian and Ryan ran near the hoop as they played an intense game of basketball with a small group of other boys. Brian and Ryan were extremely competitive. Although they were not the best basketball players in the fifth grade, they played harder than most of their peers and usually scored points during every game. The bell rang and children scattered, rushing toward the school's entrance. Brian and Ryan closed their ears to the wailing bell and continued shooting hoops. Mrs. Donaldson, Ryan's homeroom teacher, approached the boys, waving her arms.

"Boys! Time to go now!" Mrs. Donaldson screamed as she increased her walking pace to something that resembled a light jog from a distance.

Ryan darted toward the basketball hoop with the ball cradled in his arms. Brian sprinted up to him and snatched the ball away. As Brian prepared to run away, Ryan stuck out his leg, tripping him. Brian plummeted to the ground, landing on his stomach.

"Okay, this is my last warning." By now, Mrs. Donaldson's plump face appeared flustered as she huffed. "Detention if you don't come in now!"

Ryan threw the basketball into the hoop and ran into the school building.

Mrs. Donaldson peered over her oversized glasses as she leaned over, staring at Brian lying motionless on the ground. "Are you okay? You're gonna be late for class."

Brian suddenly realized that he must have blacked out for a minute. "Yeah, I just tripped."

"Well, hurry before you receive a tardy."

Brian lifted himself up and brushed dirt off his pants as he walked into the school building.

"Hey, man, you want me to do your test?" Ryan sneaked up behind Brian, whispering near his ear. Ryan's whispers were barely a whisper at all, so Brian looked around to see if someone else might have heard what he said.

Brian hesitated. "I guess. What class do you have?"

"Art. Room 201."

Mrs. Donaldson picked up her pace as she stomped down the hallway toward Ryan and Brian. "Boys! Get in class!"

"Room 215!" Brian shouted to Ryan before running down the hall into the art room. Due to the loud hallway chatter, he wasn't sure if Brian heard him. He glanced over his shoulder as he walked down the hallway and noticed that Ryan seemed to go in the right direction.

Ryan walked into room 215 and sat at the only empty

student desk. The teacher, Ms. Johnson, stood with her back to the class as she wrote on the chalkboard. After several minutes, she turned around and grabbed a stack of papers off her desk.

"Okay, class, you will have about forty-five minutes to complete the test. As a reminder, show all calculations. I need to see how you arrived at the answer. I will deduct a point for any answer that doesn't have calculations." Ms. Johnson handed out the exam packets to each student. When she reached Ryan, she stood in front of his desk staring at him instead of handing him a test.

"Tanisha, finish passing these out." Ms. Johnson then spun around and handed the remaining stack of tests to Tanisha. She pointed to Ryan. "You, follow me." Ryan hopped out of his seat and followed Ms. Johnson out of the classroom. They walked down the hallway.

Ms. Johnson stopped and peered down at Ryan. "Where are you supposed to be?"

"Art." Ms. Johnson completely surprised Ryan. He thought for sure Ms. Johnson would believe he was Brian. After all, the teachers repeatedly mixed up the brothers' names every day. Ms. Johnson walked Ryan to the art room and walked him in.

"Excuse me. You have the wrong student. Brian, come with me so you can take your test." The classroom erupted in laughter. Brian stood up and walked up to Ms. Johnson with his head held low, and Ryan quickly took a seat at his desk.

"You know, you're only punishing yourself. Now, you have even less time to finish your test, so I hope you're ready."

After class, Brian sauntered up to Ryan. "Man, what'd you do?"

"What?"

"What happened? Why didn't you take the test?"

"She wouldn't let me take it. She knew I wasn't you," Ryan said.

"How?"

"I don't know." Ryan shrugged his right shoulder.

"You must have done something wrong."

"I didn't. I just sat down like I was you." Feeling frustrated, Ryan turned his back to Brian and headed toward his locker.

James, the notorious class clown, walked up to Brian and chuckled. "Hey, I heard you got amnesia and went to the wrong class!"

Brian shoved past him. "Man, leave me alone."

"You must admit, what you did was pretty stupid. You're not even dressed alike. Hey, loser, did you really think no one would notice that you had on different colored shirts?"

"Yo, Ryan." Brian briskly walked up to Ryan. "Next

time, we should dress alike. Then, the teachers really won't be able to tell us apart."

"Man, we're not babies."

"I know, but it will work. They really won't be able to tell us apart if we look exactly alike."

"Then they'll really tease us." Ryan grabbed a book out of his locker.

"Who cares?" Brian shrugged. "That's the only way we can make it work."

"I care."

The school bell rang, and the boys speed walked their way to their next class.

After their last class, Ryan and Brian started walking home. Suddenly, there was a honking sound. As they looked up, they noticed one of their classmates, John, hanging out of a car window waving a card in his hand. "Hey, twins, come here. I have something for you," he yelled as he frantically waved his arms. Brian and Ryan were almost hit as they dashed toward the car parked across the street to see what John wanted.

"Hey, twins, I'm inviting you to my birthday party." John said, shoving the invitation toward Brian's face. "It's

Saturday. You can share the invitation. You're both invited."

John's mother rolled down the front passenger window. "Do you boys want a ride home?"

"No, thank you," Brian said as he stared at the invitation.

"Yeah, we want a ride. Come on, Brian," Ryan said as he hopped into the car. Brian climbed in behind him.

As she started the car, John's mother glanced into the rearview mirror. "Do you boys think you will be able to make it to the party? If you want, I can talk to your parents about it."

"My mom's not home," Ryan said.

"Well, let your mom and dad know I can pick you up if you need a ride. I would need to pick you up about a half hour earlier."

When the twins arrived home, they grabbed a bag of potato chips. Suddenly, a lanky man walked into the kitchen and pulled a can of beer out of the refrigerator. Ryan and Brian stared intensely at the man while munching on the chips.

"Oh, you must be Margaret's boys. I'm Charlie." Charlie opened the can of beer and chugged it. He then walked over to Brian and peered down at him. "Which one are you?"

Brian glanced at Ryan before staring at his feet. Ryan

tapped Brian's shoulder as a gesture telling him to say something.

"What's wrong with you boys? Are you some mutes? Don't ya know how to talk?"

Brian and Ryan slowly backed away from Charlie.

"It looks like I'm gonna have to teach ya'll some manners."

A door suddenly slammed, startling the twins. Brian and Ryan looked up and saw their mother, Margaret, stomping into the kitchen, her heavy feet making loud thumping sounds as she walked. Charlie approached Margaret, pulled her close, and kissed her hard on the lips. Margaret turned away from him when she looked up and saw the twins watching her.

"Boys, this is Mister Charlie. He's going to live with us."

"Oh, we already met. Do they speak 'cause they ain't said nothing."

"Boys, did you say hello to Mister Charlie?"

"Is Mister Michael still going to live here too?" Ryan popped a chip into his mouth while Brian froze as he struggled to stifle his laughter.

"What? You know... Don't you sass me! Go do your homework now!"

Brian and Ryan ran out of the kitchen and darted up the stairs to their bedroom.

Ryan ran and threw himself onto his bed. "What do you think of the new roommate?"

"He's not Dad."

"Dad's dead."

"Don't say that!" Brian picked up his pillow and threw it at Ryan.

"It's true. He can't come back. Maybe we'll get a new dad." Ryan lifted the pillow and whacked Brian with it.

"I never want a new dad," Brian said as he yanked the pillow out of Ryan's hands.

"Well, you can't have the old one back."

"Yeah, well, we don't need a new one."

"You don't think Mister Charlie would make a good dad?" Ryan teased.

"Don't even joke like that!"

Margaret walked into the twins' bedroom. Ryan hopped off his bed and quickly snatched his workbook out of his backpack. "I sure hear a lot of talkin' in here. Let me see your homework."

"We're not finished," Brian mumbled as he pulled his workbook out of his backpack and started writing.

"What was that? I know you didn't say what I thought you said."

"Mom, can we go to John's birthday party?" Ryan asked as he tapped his pencil on his workbook.

"When is it?"

"Saturday," Brian said.

"This Saturday? You know I work."

"His mom can pick us up," Ryan chimed in.

"Let's see. Homework incomplete, chores not done, and now you wanna party?"

"Please, can we go? We'll do our homework and chores. Please?" Ryan whined.

"I don't know John. I don't know John's mother. You know how I feel about you going to people's houses without me. You're not going."

"Aww, we never get to go to parties or have friends." Ryan never understood why his mother refused to allow him to visit his classmates. She often hinted that something terrible happened to her as a child while visiting a friend, but she refused to provide any details to the twins.

"You're lucky. You don't need to go to a party or worry about making friends. You have a great lifelong best friend to hang out with. I wish I had a twin like you. Now, get back to that homework!"

After his mother left the room, Brian pulled a tattered picture of his father out of his pocket. He really missed his father and still did not fully understand what cancer was or how it caused his father to die. Everything was so different when he was alive. As soon as his father came home from work, he played games with him and Ryan. Their father spent every weekend teaching them how to shoot hoops and throw a pitch. Also, his mother only worked part-time and was always home when he came home from school. Everything seemed so perfect back then.

Suddenly, Brian felt a tug at his picture as Ryan yanked it out of his hand. "What are you looking at?" Ryan asked as he glanced at the picture and hopped onto his bed.

"Hey, give that back!" Brian ran over to Ryan and snatched the picture away from him.

Ryan leaned back against his pillow, closed his eyes, and thought about his favorite memory of his father. It was his last Little League game. Ryan was pitching, and the other team was at bat. It was the bottom of the ninth inning, and the twins' team was winning by one run. The opposing team had the bases loaded and only one out. The other team's best player, who had already hit five home runs, was up to bat. Ryan's fingers trembled, and the ground seemed to shake beneath him as he stared the batter in the eyes. Suddenly, Ryan heard his father cheering, and he took a deep breath as his body steadied.

Ryan turned and glanced at Brian, who was playing first base and waiting for their secret play signal. Ryan briefly looked at third base and then straight at the batter as he gave the secret signal to Brian. Seconds later, Ryan did a windup and threw the trickiest changeup he had ever thrown. The speed and change of the ball confused the batter just enough, and he sent the ball in a line drive toward Ryan. Ryan caught the ball to secure out number two and quickly slung the ball to Brian at first base. The crowd roared as the other team's runner tried to beat the ball back to the base. Brian reached up and caught the ball and tagged the runner just in time. The twins had successfully executed the changeup, and it led to the double play that won the game. Their father passed away two weeks later, and they were too distraught to continue playing Little League, but they were happy their father got to see them win a game.

The bedroom door flung open. "I know you're not sleeping without that homework being done," Margaret said, looking at the twins.

Startled, Ryan hopped up off the bed. "No. Just thinking. I wasn't asleep." Ryan yanked a book out of his backpack and began studying its contents.

After standing in the doorway for several minutes, Margaret left, satisfied that the twins were completing their homework assignments.

SEVEN YEARS LATER - HIGH SCHOOL

Loud chatter filled the air as hundreds of teenagers crowded the hallway and shot off in different directions.

Brian and Ryan dashed into the boys' locker room and passed rows of lockers until they saw an empty row. They went to the empty row and plopped their backpacks onto the bench. Since there were other students in the locker room, Ryan and Brian spoke in a tone slightly above a whisper.

"It's so nice to only have one exam to study for. I'm going to ace our math tests." Ryan pulled his blue shirt off over his lanky body and grabbed the green one stashed in his backpack.

"Yeah, well, make sure you do something a little different on my test, like make a mistake so he won't be suspicious. Next time, I want to do the math tests, and you do science." Brian slipped a blue shirt, identical to the one Ryan took off, over his head. He stuffed the green shirt he had just removed into his backpack.

"Man, don't you flunk my science test!" Ryan exclaimed.

"When was the last time I flunked? Make sure you don't flunk my math test."

"I'm just sayin' you better not flunk. One mistake, that's all."

Brian and Ryan left the locker room and hurried to their respective classes. After class, Ryan saw one of his crushes, Kira, strutting down the hall. Kira was the most stylish girl in the school with clothes that looked like they came straight off the runway, and her cocoa brown skin was as smooth as butter. Every day, she styled her hair in a completely different look whether she was sporting braids, twists, or her kinky curls.

"Hey, Kira, I like your afro puffs. What time do you want me to pick you up for the prom?"

"Um, who are you?" Kira said as she rolled her eyes.

"Surely, you remember the name Ryan Wright. What say you, prom date?" Ryan asked as he wrapped his arm around Kira's shoulder.

Kira shoved Ryan's arm away and stepped aside. "Oh, you look so much like another guy I know. I believe his name is Brian. Do you know him?"

"Oh, so you have jokes now." Ryan chuckled. "You still didn't answer my—"

"Kira, is twin boy harassing you?" Kira's best friend, Jasmine, stepped between Ryan and Kira. "And no, she does not want to go to prom with you."

"Of course, she doesn't want to go to the prom with him because she's going with me," Brian exclaimed.

"You're both wrong," Kira said.

"Yeah, she's going to the prom with Jason, so you're both out of luck." Jasmine grabbed Kira's arm and pulled her away from the twins.

Kira leaned close to Jasmine and whispered. "Why did

you tell that lie?" Jasmine laughed as she walked down the hallway to her class.

The school bell rang, and the students scurried away to their classes. After class, Brian and Ryan met by the lockers.

"Man, what was that about?"

"What do you mean?" Brian turned away from Ryan as he opened his locker.

"You know what I'm talking about. I asked Kira to the prom first!"

"Yeah, and she said 'no.' I was just kidding anyway. If she said no to you, I knew she would say no to me too," Brian said.

"Well, I haven't given up yet."

"In that case, neither have I!" Brian chuckled as he grabbed a book out of his locker. "Anyway, didn't Jasmine say she already has a date?"

"There's plenty of time for her to change her mind. I'm not too worried about that."

Early the next morning, Brian snuck into his neighbor's yard and picked some of her best flowers. He gently slipped the flowers into his backpack and returned home. Prior to leaving for school, Brian sat at the kitchen table and wrote a note to Kira, signed "from a secret admirer." While Brian was writing the note, Ryan sauntered into the kitchen and wiggled his nose.

"It smells like flowers in here. What are you doing?"

"Nothing. Let's go before we're late." Brian quickly folded and stuffed the note into his backpack, and the twins left for school. Upon arriving at school, Brian walked and stood near Kira's locker. When the bell rang, he looked around to make sure that no one was looking in his direction. Then, he quickly removed the flowers and note from his backpack and set them on the floor in front of Kira's locker.

Later that day, as Ryan and Brian walked toward the exit after their last class, Kira approached the twins. The flowers were sticking out of her unzipped bag.

"Hey, Ryan, can we talk privately?"

Ryan turned toward Kira. "Of course. Brian, you go ahead. I'll meet you outside." As Brian walked away, he continuously looked back at Ryan and Kira.

Kira stepped closer to Ryan. "First, I would like to thank you."

"Thank me? Well, I don't know what I did, but you are welcome."

Kira giggled. "Oh, and you're modest too. Anyway, I was thinking about what you said yesterday."

"Oh, what was that?"

"About the prom. I was thinking maybe I could use a date. Do you know anyone who might be available to take me to the prom?"

"I'm definitely available."

"Cool."

Ryan grinned. "So, you're going to the prom with me?"

Kira giggled. "Sure, I guess I'll go to prom with you. I mean I don't have another date, so I might as well go with you."

"Cool. Let's exchange numbers." Ryan yanked a piece of paper out of his notebook, wrote down his phone number, and handed it to Kira. Kira tore a corner off the paper, wrote her phone number on the torn corner, and handed it to Ryan. After Kira walked away, Ryan jogged outside and found Brian.

"What did Kira want?"

"Oh, nothing really," Ryan said airily. "She just wanted to talk about going to the prom with yours truly."

"She's going to the prom with you?"

"Yeah, she's my prom date." Ryan smiled and danced during his next three steps.

"I wonder why she decided to go with you instead of me."

"Because she knows I'm the better twin." Ryan chuckled.

"I wonder if it's because of the flowers I gave her."

"She didn't say anything about flowers. Besides, I

asked her to the prom yesterday. This has nothing to do with you."

"I left some flowers at her locker this morning," Brian exclaimed.

"And what is your point? Obviously, you didn't impress her with those flowers."

Three months later, Ryan prepared for the prom. He put on his tuxedo and stood in front of the bathroom mirror making sure that everything looked perfect. He stared at his light brown skin, green eyes, and short, wavy, sandy brown hair. As Ryan gazed at his reflection, Brian walked into the bathroom.

"Are you sure you don't want to go to the prom? You don't need a date."

"I don't have a ticket. Besides, I don't want to be a third wheel even though you stole my date."

"She was never your date." Ryan brushed his hair and practiced smiling in front of the mirror. "In fact, I should be mad at you for tryin' to steal my date after I asked her first."

"Anyway, I didn't rent a tuxedo like you."

"This is our last year. If you want to go to the prom, I'll make sure you go to the prom. I'm sure I can figure out a way to sneak you in. If that doesn't work, we can switch clothes for a little while. You can go in, dance a couple of dances, and take a few pictures. Then, return home while I finish out the night with my superhot date." Ryan picked up his camera off the bathroom counter and handed it to Brian. "Here, take my picture."

Brian took four pictures of Ryan as he posed. "Maybe I will think about going."

"Okay, if you go, meet me at nine o'clock in the men's bathroom. Make sure you wear a suit so you don't stand out too much. If there's a family restroom, we'll go in there to exchange clothes."

"Okay."

"Why didn't you ask someone else to the prom?"

"I really only like Kira."

"Oh, well. Your loss. Hey, the limo will be here soon. I can't wait."

"If I do decide to go, I guess I can borrow mom's car."

Thirty minutes later, the limo arrived. As Ryan walked to the limousine, his mother and Brian stood outside taking pictures of Ryan. Then, Ryan rode the limousine to Kira's house while the twins' mother and Brian followed closely behind in their mother's car. As Ryan walked up to Kira's house and rang her doorbell, Brian and his mother waited outside by the car. Kira's father opened the door, and Ryan strolled into the home. "Hello, young man. You make sure you don't keep her out too late."

Kira's mom smiled and walked over to Ryan and took a picture of him. "You look very handsome. Kira, your date's here." Kira walked down the stairs wearing a beautiful gold, body-hugging dress that flowed down to her ankles. Her dark brown hair was styled in long spiral curls, and her dark brown skin glistened. "Hi, Ryan," Kira said as she smiled.

"Okay, you two, stand over here." Kira's mother motioned to the bottom of the stairs. "Get next to each other. I want to get some pictures." Everyone walked outside, and Kira's parents greeted Brian and his mother. Brian remained standing next to his mother's car while his mother snapped pictures of Ryan and Kira. Brian was mesmerized by Kira's beauty and stared at her while she posed for pictures.

Suddenly, Brian felt someone tapping on his shoulder. "Okay, now let me get some pictures of my boys. Go stand over by your brother." Brian did not feel like smiling or posing, but he stood next to Ryan while his mother took several pictures as she beamed with pride.

Kira's father also took group pictures of everyone, including the twins' mother and Brian. Then, he firmly shook Ryan's hand. "Make sure you take care of Kira and make sure you're back before midnight."

After Ryan and Kira finished posing for pictures, they hopped into the limo and rode to the prom. At the prom, Ryan and Kira ate dinner and danced. They also posed for pictures with the professional prom photographer. At nine o'clock, Ryan excused himself to go to the bathroom, and Kira walked over to a small group of her friends and started talking to them.

Ryan walked to the men's room and called out Brian's name. As he exited the men's room, he saw Brian walking toward him.

"Hey. Follow me. I saw a family bathroom around the corner." Ryan and Brian walked to the family bathroom, where they exchanged clothes. "Oh, don't forget this." Ryan slipped an orange wristband off his wrist and handed it to Brian. "You'll need it to get in."

"Okay, thanks."

"Remember, don't stay there for too long. Dance a couple of songs, take a few pictures, sip some punch, and meet me back here. You should be able to do all that in a half hour."

Brian looked over at Ryan. "I can tell you've been dancing a lot with all that sweat. Maybe I need to toss some water on myself."

"Whatever. Just hurry back."

Brian handed a key to Ryan. "Here, hold onto the car key for me."

Brian held his hands under the faucet and caught some water. Then, he used both of his hands to flick some of the water over his head and walked out of the bathroom. Ryan left the bathroom a few minutes later and walked outside.

Brian sauntered into the ballroom where the prom was being held and looked for Kira. He did not see her, so he walked over to the punch bowl and picked up a cup off the table. Kira snuck up behind Brian.

"Hey, handsome. This is my favorite song." Kira grabbed Brian's hand, and they walked to the dance floor. After dancing for three songs, Brian and Kira went to the photo booth and posed for pictures. Kira's friend Jasmine walked up to the photo booth.

"Hey, guys, let me get some pictures of you."

Kira and Brian posed for pictures while Jasmine snapped her camera. "Hey, Ryan, where's your brother?" Jasmine asked. Brian wrapped his arms around Kira waiting for Jasmine to take their picture. "Earth to Ryan. Where's Brian? You know, your brother?"

"Huh? Oh, um, he's not here."

"Girl, Brian did not come to the prom. Are you done taking pictures? I'm ready to head back to the dance floor," Kira said as she grabbed Brian's hand.

"Yeah, just one more." Jasmine took another picture of Kira and Brian.

"Hey, get one with my camera too." Kira handed her

camera to Jasmine, and Jasmine used it to take two pictures of Kira and Brian.

After taking the pictures, Kira and Brian walked to the dance floor and danced to a slow song. At the end of the song, Brian leaned forward and kissed Kira gently on the lips. Kira blushed as she smiled and kissed him back.

Brian grinned. "This has been the best night of my life."

"Yeah, me too."

Ryan frantically paced outside the ballroom as he continuously checked the time on his watch. More than one hour had passed, and Brian still had not returned. Ryan walked up to the ballroom entrance and peeked in. A prom chaperone approached Ryan. "Wristband?"

"What?"

"Where's your wristband?"

"Oh, I must have lost it." Ryan nervously glanced at his wrist.

"No wristband, no entry."

Ryan stepped away from the ballroom and sauntered over to the bathroom door, where he stood waiting for Brian to return. After ten minutes passed, the prom chaperone approached him. "Maybe you should just leave. If you think you're gonna just sneak in there, you got the wrong idea."

Ryan swallowed the hard lump in his throat as beads

of sweat began to roll down his forehead. "But my brother. I'm waiting—"

"Don't make me get security!"

Ryan darted out of the building and searched for his mother's car in the parking lot. After locating the car, he entered it, slammed the door, and waited. He didn't really know what he was waiting for. After all, Brian had no idea he was waiting in the car, and the prom was almost over. He thought about going to the limo and waiting for Kira there, but what would she think if she saw him there? Ryan could not believe his brother would steal his prom date and his whole prom experience. After thirty minutes passed, Ryan drove home.

Two hours later, the limousine dropped Brian off at home. When Brian walked into the home, Ryan ran and tackled him to the floor. Brian punched Ryan in the nose, and Ryan returned the punch, striking Brian in the side of his face. Brian stood up and ran his hands over his face, feeling for blood.

"I can't believe you! You ruined my night." Ryan lunged forward and pushed Brian's shoulders, forcing him to crash onto the floor.

"I looked for you." Brian kneeled briefly and slowly stood up.

"Quit lying. I waited over an hour. All you had to do was leave when you were supposed to leave. I was nice to you. I let you have a prom moment. And what did I get in return? You stole my prom from me."

"Okay, I admit I was late, but I looked for you."

"What the hell is going on down there? What's all that noise?" the twins' mother yelled at the top of the stairs. "Don't make me come down there!"

"We don't want to get in trouble. Let's not say anything," Brian whispered as he walked toward the kitchen to get a napkin to wipe his face.

"Sorry, ma. We'll be quiet. We were just talking about prom," Ryan said, looking up the stairs.

"You boys get to bed. It's after two o'clock in the morning."

Brian walked over to Ryan, dabbing his face with the napkin.

"Don't worry. It doesn't look too bad."

"I'm really sorry, man. I just lost track of time, and I did look for you. I really did. Forgive me?" Brian pushed his fist toward Ryan. "Brothers forever."

Ryan grinned and fist-bumped Brian. "Forever brothers."

THREE

Brian and Ryan were accepted into five colleges and won full academic scholarships to all five schools. Their mother was so proud of their academic achievements that she gifted them a used car to share as a graduation gift after saving money for an entire year to buy it.

Brian registered for classes at Stanford University while Ryan registered for classes at University of California, Berkeley. Throughout his younger years, Ryan often imagined what his college life would be like. Hanging out with Brian, studying with Brian, and saving time and energy by taking tests for each other. It was always great to only need to study for half of his classes because he had a brother who could take some of his exams. Brian would take the math tests while he took the science tests. Yes, Ryan had everything planned until reality hit. He was excited about the chance for a new experience, but how would he survive with Brian at a different college? He had never spent a single day separated from his brother, and he wasn't sure that he could survive college life without seeing him every day.

Despite attending different colleges, the twins succeeded in seeing each other almost every weekend. They even made sure that they registered for many of the same classes. If the same class was not offered at both schools, they registered for similar classes.

One day, as Ryan was leaving his intermediate-level Spanish class, a young woman named Amanda approached him.

"Are you ready for next week's exam?" Amanda stepped in front of Ryan and smiled, stopping him in his tracks. He looked down and saw a petite buxom blonde staring up at him smiling.

"Not yet, but I plan to study all weekend."

"Well, some of us are getting together for a study group on Saturday at four o'clock. We're going to meet in a group study room at the library. The room is reserved under my name, Amanda Johnson. Feel free to stop by."

"Thanks. I will keep that in mind. My brother is supposed to come for a visit this weekend, but maybe he can skip this weekend. Or maybe he can come to the study group too. He's also taking a Spanish class, but at a different college."

"You and your brother sound really close."

"Yeah, actually, we're twins," Ryan said with a grin.

"Cool. I'm surprised you don't go to the same college. He didn't want to go to the best school in California?"

"Well, he goes to Stanford. That's a good school too. We were going to attend the same school, but we thought it would be cool to see how singletons get to live life."

"Interesting. So, do you look alike?"

"We're identical. Brian, that's my brother. He's about a half inch shorter, but otherwise people really can't tell us apart."

"So, your brother is Brian, but what's your name?"

"Oh, I'm sorry. My name is Ryan."

"So, how do I know you're really Ryan and not your brother Brian?" Amanda smiled and winked.

Ryan laughed. "I guess you'll just have to take me for my word. Hey, I'm going to grab a bite to eat at the cafeteria. Do you want to join me?"

"Sure. I was on my way there anyway."

Ryan and Amanda walked to the cafeteria together. After purchasing food, they sat at a table at the back of the cafeteria.

Amanda took a sip of water. "This may be a weird question, but have you ever considered modeling?"

"No, I can definitely say I've never considered that. Why do you ask?"

"Well, my sister works as a scout for a modeling agency. You seem to have certain qualities she said she looks for in a recruit. Tall, well-toned body; smooth, clear, tanned skin; razor-sharp cheekbones; and gorgeous, green eyes."

Ryan blushed. "I've definitely never been interested in doing anything like that."

"Well, I'm just telling you because it might be a good way to make money while attending college, and it's not something you would do every day. And I'm no expert, but I think you would be very marketable. You have a look that would work for companies looking for several different ethnicities. Maybe your brother could do it too since he's your twin and looks just like you."

Ryan sighed. "I don't know. That doesn't even sound fun or interesting."

"Does a job have to be fun? You might get to travel around the world. Wouldn't that be interesting? Besides, it can be a temporary way to make some money to pay your tuition."

"Who said I have to pay tuition? I might have a full scholarship."

"Well, even if you have a scholarship, it might be nice to have some extra money."

"I'll think about it."

"Can I give your number to my sister?" Amanda pouted and pleaded with her eyes.

Ryan yanked a piece of paper out of his backpack and jotted his name and number on it. He slid the paper across the table to Amanda.

"Thank you. She'll be in touch." Amanda smiled as she picked up the paper. She folded the paper and it placed it into her purse.

Later that evening, Ryan rummaged through his cluttered closet looking for his favorite pair of jeans when one of his prom photos dropped to the floor. As he picked up the picture, he thought about Kira. He really believed they'd have ended up in a serious relationship if they had attended the same college. Ryan decided to give her a call.

"Hey, Ryan. What are you up to?" she asked.

"Just studying. Hey, when are you coming back to Cali for a visit?" Ryan inquired.

"I might head that way during break. Hey, I have to go. I'm on my way to class."

"Okay, well, don't be a stranger," he said. "Maybe when you come to town, we can get together."

Kira giggled. "Sounds like a plan."

After ending the call, Ryan smiled. Several minutes later, he received a call from an unknown number.

"Hello."

"Hi, may I please speak to Ryan?"

"This is Ryan."

"Hi, Ryan. My name is Elise. You spoke with my sister, Amanda, about possibly doing some modeling."

"She mentioned it, but I haven't really decided if that's something I want to do."

"Well, maybe we can meet in person and I can see if you might be a good fit with my agency. At that time, we'll take a few pictures and I will explain the different types of modeling and answer your questions. There is absolutely no obligation on your part."

Ryan hesitated. "Sure, I guess that will be okay, as long as there's no obligation."

"No obligation. Are you available this weekend? I can meet you on campus if you prefer."

"Sure, but it doesn't have to be on campus. I have the car this weekend. I share it with my brother," Ryan said.

"Cool. Well, is it okay if I text you the address and directions?"

"Sure."

"And does Saturday at noon work for you?"

"Yeah, that would be great."

On Saturday, Ryan drove to the modeling agency and met with Elise and the agent, Beth. Beth had Ryan fill out an application, which included questions about his height and weight. Then she had him stand against a blank white wall while she took pictures of him. After taking pictures, they went into Beth's office and sat down.

"Ryan, I like what I see. There are different types of models, but I believe you would do great with both print and runway. You have the right look and the right height and weight for what we are looking for. Do you have any questions for me?"

"Well, how much is involved? I'm in college."

"As much or as little as you want. If someone is looking for a model for a particular campaign, I tell you when and where you need to go. If you're unavailable, just let me know. Of course, I'll want you to do as much as possible because if you don't work, I don't get paid. For the best chance of success, you will need a portfolio. I want to schedule you an appointment with a photographer so we can have a modeling portfolio made for you. There are no up-front costs. We will deduct the portfolio expense from your first paycheck. If you're interested, you can read over the agency contract and return a signed copy to me." Beth slid a copy of the contract across her desk to Ryan. "If you sign up, I will also have you attend a couple of my free runway and audition workshops."

After Ryan left the modeling agency, he got a call from Amanda.

"Hey, Ryan. This is Amanda. Congratulations! My sister told me the good news."

"Thank you."

"Let's go celebrate. My treat. What's your favorite restaurant?"

"Um, I don't know. You don't need to treat me to dinner. I was going to head to the cafeteria in a little while."

"I insist. I know about a great Italian restaurant that just opened. Don't tell me you love the cafeteria food so much that you want to pass up the chance to eat some great food at a great restaurant."

"I guess you have a point," he said. "Okay, let's meet up in an hour."

When Ryan arrived at the restaurant, he saw Amanda standing by the hostess stand. She was wearing a pretty, floral minidress paired with red stilettos. Amanda gave Ryan a hug, and the two of them were seated a few minutes later.

"So, tell me more about yourself," Amanda said.

"What do you want to know?"

"Everything." Amanda giggled. "Seriously, what do you do for fun?"

"Actually, that's a good question. I haven't had much fun lately, but I enjoy watching sports, working out, and going out dancing."

"Well, it looks like we have something in common,"

she said. "I like dancing too. When was the last time you went out dancing?"

Ryan paused. "The last time I went dancing was prom."

Amanda laughed. "Really? Did you have a nice time at prom?"

"I did until my brother stole my date."

Amanda scrunched up her nose. "Ouch. That's not cool."

"Yeah, well, it was partly my fault. I let him dance with her."

"Well, if you were my prom date, I wouldn't have let your brother steal me away. Maybe we can go dancing one day. Do you think you can break away one evening to go dancing with me?"

"I think I might be able to find some time for dancing."

One month later, Ryan received a call about a modeling job that required him to fly to Chicago on a Friday. However, his final exam was scheduled on the same Friday, so he called his brother.

Brian picked up. "Hey, bro, what's going on?"

"Are you busy Friday?"

Brian paused. He pondered potential excuses because there was a good chance Ryan wanted him to do something he did not want to do. However, he also knew

Ryan's persuasiveness would ultimately force him to agree. "Maybe. Why do you want to know?"

"Remember when I told you about the modeling agency? Well, they called me about a gig in Chicago on Friday."

"You want me to go to Chicago with you?"

"Actually, I was hoping you could go to Chicago instead of me. I have a final exam Friday. There is no way I can reschedule it, and the job pays a lot of money plus travel."

"I don't know anything about modeling. Also, I'm a half inch shorter than you. I'm sure they'll notice something."

"They won't know anything. They only saw a few pictures of me. It's not like they met me in person. I only met the agent in person. You can put on some shoes with a higher sole or something. I also heard about something you can put inside your shoe to make you look a little taller. I think they're called lift insoles or something like that. Honestly, I really don't think anyone will notice the slight height difference."

"I don't know. That sounds like a disaster just waiting to happen. At least you went to a modeling class. I don't know anything about modeling. Why can't you just tell them you're unavailable? Surely they don't expect a college student to be available one hundred percent of the time."

Brian opened his laptop and searched for information about modeling.

"I might have told the agent I would be available. I completely forgot about the test, and I was so excited when she sent over the contract. I signed it right away."

"You're always getting me involved in some craziness. If I say no, then what are you going to do?"

"You're not going to say no, are you? I mean you never say no. I'm sure you can find some information about how to model online. I will even let you keep all the money. They automatically deposit payments into my bank account, but I can write you a check. I'll drop off my ID to you tomorrow so you'll have it in case they ask," Ryan said.

"Well, in case I decide to do it, how much money are we talking about?"

"Fifteen hundred dollars plus travel expenses."

"Okay, just this one time. At least if I mess up terribly, they will think it's you, so I don't have to worry about my reputation." Brian chuckled.

"Thanks, man. I owe you one."

"No, you owe me a million. Now that I think about it, I do have a test next week. Maybe you can take that test for me since I'll be too busy modeling to study. I'll drop off the information when I pick up your ID."

"Okay, but we're keeping the test-taking schedule, aren't we? You're still doing my calculus test next month?"

Brian sighed. "Yeah, we can keep the rest of the schedule."

Ryan became busier as he split his time between his college studies and modeling. He also maintained regular study sessions with Amanda, and the two began spending more and more time with each other. Ryan even invited Amanda along when he visited Brian. Eventually, Ryan found himself spending so much time with Amanda that he offered most of the modeling jobs to Brian.

During his third year of college, Brian secured a summer internship at a major business consulting firm. When Brian received the internship offer letter, he decided to celebrate and called Ryan.

"Hello?"

"Hey, Ryan. Guess what happened to me today." Brian picked up the offer letter perched on his desk.

"Let's see. I'm your twin, so I guess I should be able to read your mind. Hmm. Did you get an A on your statistics midterm?"

Brian chuckled. "Unfortunately, no. Maybe I should have had you do that one for me. Anyway, I got a job." Brian started dancing and singing the words, "I got a job. I got a job."

"Does that mean you're not going to do any of the modeling for me anymore?"

"What? No. This is a summer internship that can lead

to a full-time, permanent job after graduation. You know I don't even like modeling."

"Yeah, well, the money is good."

"So, you're not going to congratulate me?"

"Congrats. Why didn't you tell me about the job? I could have applied too."

"What, you're not happy with your modeling career?"

"You know that's temporary."

"I would have told you, but I applied at the last minute, and I didn't think I would get it. Anyway, wanna come celebrate with me? There's a new club that opened near campus last week. It might be fun to check it out."

"I wish you would have told me sooner. I have a special date with Amanda planned for tonight."

"You and Amanda seem to be getting serious. Do I hear wedding bells?" Brian laughed.

"I think it's still a bit early for that."

"I don't know, you've been spending so much time together. Well, I guess I'll go clubbing by myself. Are you sure you don't wanna come? Amanda can come too. The jewelry store should be closed by then."

Ryan chuckled. "I'm sure. I'll pass this time, but let me know if you decide to go again."

Three hours later, Brian strolled three blocks to the nightclub. When he arrived at the club, there was a line a half block long filled with women in tight minidresses and men wearing their best jeans and sneakers. As he walked to the end of the line, he felt someone tap his shoulder.

"Hey, stranger."

Brian swung around to see Kira. For the first time, Brian believed in fate. It was as if everything in the universe aligned to bring the woman of his dreams to him. What were the odds? "Wow, I can't believe it. Kira, how are you? What are you doing here?" Brian reached out and hugged her.

"I came to have some fun. What have you been up to? Wait, is it Ryan or Brian?"

"What? You can't tell?" Brian chuckled. "I'm just messing with you. I'm Brian." Brian hugged Kira. "It's good to see you. What have you been up to?"

"Well, I go to Howard University. I'm home visiting during the break, so I decided to meet up with a few friends at this club. So, what are you up to these days?"

"School, like you, except I'm at Stanford, and thanks to my brother, I occasionally model."

Kira's eyes widened. "Wow, a model. That's cool. I can't say I'm completely surprised. So, how's your brother?"

"He's doing well. In fact, he hasn't said anything, but I think he's getting ready to propose to his girlfriend."

"Oh, wow, Ryan's getting engaged already? He doesn't waste much time, does he? The last time I talked to him, it was just a brief call because I was on my way to class. I guess we both have been too busy to keep in touch." Kira reached down and pulled her cell phone out of her purse. "Excuse me." She read some of her text messages.

"Is something wrong?"

"Oh, no. My friends said they were running late. It doesn't look like they'll be here for another hour."

Brian chuckled. "Well, that's great."

"It is?" Kira scrunched her eyebrows.

"Of course. It will give us a chance to spend some time catching up. Hey, why don't we go to that coffee shop across the street and wait until your friends make it to the club? We can have a coffee or espresso or whatever drink you like and chat without loud music blasting our ear drums out. It might be easier if you have them meet you at the coffee shop anyway. Then we can walk over to the club together."

"What makes you think I want to spend my night talking to you?"

"If you don't want to talk, you don't have to. We can just sit at the table staring at each other." Brian chuckled.

"Well, I guess it might be easier to listen for a phone call or text message in the coffee shop, and the nightclub is really dark."

"Yeah, so are you ready to walk over there?"

"Okay, let me send a text to my friends." Kira sent a

text message to her friends while she and Brian walked across the street to the coffee shop. "I can't believe I'm actually having coffee with a supermodel." Kira winked at Brian.

"I don't exactly qualify for supermodel status, but thanks anyway."

Coffee in hand, the pair sat at a small table near the window.

"I can't believe how much time has passed. So, you mentioned Ryan's soon-to-be fiancée. What about you? Where's your fiancée?" Kira sipped some of her coffee and glanced down at her phone to see if her friends had sent a message yet.

"I don't have one yet, but I'm hoping to eventually have one named Kira one day."

Kira giggled. "So, how many Kiras do you know?"

"You are the one and only."

"Well, you better get out there and meet some more if you plan to marry one of them one day!"

Kira's friends finally arrived at the coffee shop, and the group walked over to the nightclub together. Brian spent most of the night dancing with Kira. At the end of the evening, Kira and Brian exchanged phone numbers and gave each other a hug.

"What do you think Ryan will say when you tell him you danced with his prom date?"

Brian chuckled. "Well, it won't be the first time."

"What's that supposed to mean?"

"I'm messing with you. He missed out. It doesn't matter anyway. He has a girlfriend." Brian felt guilty about not telling Kira about taking Ryan's place at the prom. Could she understand? Would she ever speak to him again? He was sure he would tell her the truth one day after they'd developed a much deeper relationship. He imagined her laughing about the switch and wondering how she hadn't realized what happened.

Despite their busy schedules, Kira and Brian continued to communicate with each other daily through phone and video calls or text messages. Whenever Ryan received a modeling job anywhere near Washington, D.C., Brian offered to take the job so he could visit Kira. One day, just before Brian flew to visit Kira, Ryan placed a video call to him.

"Hey, Brian, are you sure you want to go to D.C. this time? I was thinking it might be good if I went instead."

"Oh, that's okay. I don't mind going."

"The reason I ask is because I was thinking about catching up with Kira and seeing what she's up to," Ryan said.

"No need for that. I've been in touch with Kira. I was planning to visit her when I got to D.C."

"Why didn't you tell me you were in touch? I thought we had no secrets," Ryan said.

"Every time I thought about telling you, we started talking about something else. Besides, aren't you busy with Amanda? You don't want to ruin things with her by running off to visit Kira."

"Well, what if I do?"

"Then you'll have me and Amanda to deal with."

Ryan scrunched his brows. "You?"

Brian looked at his brother. He said nothing more, but they shared a look; there was an understanding between them.

Four

Two years after graduating from college, Brian and Kira got married and celebrated with guests at their wedding reception. The happy couple sat at a sweetheart table while their guests sat at nearby tables surrounding them. The wedding party included Ryan and his wife of two years, Amanda; Kira's best friend, Jasmine; and Brian's friend and co-worker, Adam. Brian stood up.

"Good evening, everyone. I would like to thank all of you for celebrating this wonderful occasion with me." Brian raised his champagne glass. "Now, my brother has a few words he would like to say." Ryan stood and walked to the podium.

"I am so happy for my brother and his beautiful new wife, Kira. Brian, you have been everything to me. For my entire life, you have been my best friend, my confidant, the yin to my yang, my partner in crime, and my everything. I wish you all the happiness in the world. I know you will make a great husband because you are a lot like me." Everyone in the room laughed. "Kira, you are a wonderful woman. Brian and I have known you for a long time. I know you will take good care of Brian and keep him out of trouble."

Brian jumped up. "Hey, you're the one who needs to be kept out of trouble!"

Jasmine stumbled to the podium. "Kira and Brian, I wish you all the best. Kira, you're my girl. I have known you for ten years, and I look forward to the next ten years. Brian, you seem like a nice enough guy. You take care of my girl, Kira. Kira, if he causes any problems for you, you call me." Jasmine raised her champagne glass. "Okay, now let's get this party started!"

Ryan's wife, Amanda, approached the podium. "Congratulations, Brian and Kira! Although I have only known both of you for a few years, I know you are a great couple with every quality needed for long-term marital bliss."

Servers brought out food for everyone. After dinner, the DJ played music, and everyone danced all evening. Toward the end of the evening, Brian and Ryan performed a choreographed twin dance. At the end of the dance, Amanda darted over to Brian, stumbling along the way, grabbed him, and kissed him hard on the lips. Brian shoved her away as Kira raced over to them.

"What are you doing?" Kira asked.

"What's wrong?" Amanda felt a little woozy as she swung around and faced Kira. She suddenly realized she may have had a little too much to drink.

"You just kissed my husband. Your husband is that one, the one with the green tie." Kira pointed to Ryan, who was standing next to Brian.

Amanda's face turned beet red. "Oh, I'm sorry. I'm so sorry. I didn't... They look so much alike. I'm so sorry. I'm really sorry, Kira. Sorry, Brian." Amanda darted out of the ballroom, and Ryan followed her out. The roar of laughter echoed throughout the room. The remaining wedding guests filtered out of the ballroom, filling their chatter with discussions about what Amanda had done.

Brian and Kira arrived at the Hawaiian resort where they would spend the next two weeks for their honeymoon. Ryan and his wife joined them on the trip. The couples rented adjoining villas in a luxury resort in Wailea, Maui. Palm trees swayed and, brightly colored hibiscus beckoned. Both villas were oceanfront and abutted a long, white sandy beach. After checking in, the couples headed to their respective villas.

Kira and Brian toured their spacious villa. After the short tour, Kira plopped down onto the sofa.

"I told Ryan we would meet them for dinner at five o'clock," said Brian as he sat down next to Kira. She laid her head on his shoulder.

"I'm so tired." Kira's eyes felt heavier with each passing minute. She struggled to keep them open and repeatedly opened them seconds after letting them fall shut.

"Why don't you take a nap? I'll join you and set my alarm."

Kira raised her arms over her head and giggled. "Okay, I'm ready for you to carry me over the threshold now."

"Where's the threshold?" Brian chuckled.

"I'm sure you'll figure it out. Come on, I'm waiting. My arms are getting tired."

Brian picked Kira up, almost dropping her as he lifted her into his arms. "It's just jet lag. I've been working hard building up these muscles for this very moment." Brian kissed Kira on the lips as he lifted her and slowly carried her to the bedroom. By the time Brian reached the bedroom, Kira had dozed off.

Brian set the alarm on the clock on the nightstand and climbed into bed next to Kira. After two hours, the alarm wailed, and Brian sat up and slapped off the alarm clock with his hand. Meanwhile, Kira was completely motionless. Brian attempted to awaken Kira by tapping on her shoulders and gently nudging her. When that didn't work, he tickled her.

"Ooh, if you don't stop that, I'm gonna get you!" Kira pushed Brian toward the edge of the bed with her legs.

"What are you going to get me, a gift?" Brian chuckled. "Aren't you hungry?"

"Okay, let's take a quick shower before we go."

After showering, Kira and Brian walked to the resort's restaurant to meet Amanda and Brian. When they arrived at the restaurant, they saw Amanda and Brian sitting at a table.

"Hey, guys." Brian hugged Ryan and Amanda and sat at the table with them.

Amanda glanced up at Brian as he sat down. Then she turned toward Ryan. "Ryan, don't you have that exact same shirt? I think I remember seeing it in the suitcase."

"Oh, yeah. A lot of our clothes are the same. We have the same style."

"Yeah, even when we don't shop together, we end up with the same clothes," Brian exclaimed as he perused the menu.

Amanda turned toward Ryan. "You're not planning on dressing alike while on vacation, are you?" Amanda inquired.

"We stopped doing that a long time ago," Ryan said.

"Oh, yeah, you don't have to worry about that. I don't even think I saw them dress alike in high school."

Amanda grinned. "So, what were they like in high school? Did they prank everyone?"

"Hon, why would you even ask that? You know me," Ryan said as he shoved a piece of bacon into his mouth.

"That's why I asked, because I know you."

"Oh, no. You must have me confused with someone else." Ryan chuckled. "Honeymooners, what are your plans for tomorrow?"

"Well, we have a couple's spa package booked for tomorrow morning. That's all we have planned for tomorrow. We'll spend most of the day lounging and hanging out at the beach. Now, the day after tomorrow, we plan to do some shopping, and then, we booked a dinner cruise."

"Oh, why didn't you tell us about the dinner cruise? We could have joined you."

Brian chuckled. "What makes you think we want a third and fourth wheel—no offense, Amanda—on our honeymoon?"

"Brian!" Kira poked her husband.

"Don't you want some alone time?" Brian nudged Kira.

"If you were that concerned with alone time, you

wouldn't have invited your brother and his wife on the honeymoon with us," Kira said.

"You'll be on a cruise with a lot of other people you don't even know," Ryan exclaimed.

Kira leaned toward Ryan. "Ryan, I'm sure it's not too late for you to sign up for the dinner cruise if you really want to go. Brian and I will make sure we have plenty of alone time."

After dinner, Kira and Brian strolled on the beach before heading to bed. The next morning, Brian and Ryan met for an early morning jog before their wives woke up. As the twins finished their morning run, Brian's phone rang, and he answered it.

"Hey, Brian, where are you?"

"Oh, Ryan and I decided to go out for a morning run. You were still asleep."

Kira sighed. "Well, we have a couple's spa appointment this morning."

"I'm on my way back."

When Ryan and Brian reached their cluster of villas, they saw Amanda walking in their direction carrying a cup of coffee.

"Hi, Amanda," Brian and Ryan said simultaneously.

"Oh, hi. Where were you two?"

"We just went out for a morning run," Brian said.

"Oh, okay." Amanda squinted her eyes slightly. With a

confused look, she glanced at Ryan and then at Brian. "Well, I just went out for some coffee." Amanda continued to look at the twins with a confused look.

"Is something wrong?" Ryan asked.

"Okay, which one of you is Ryan?"

"That would be me," Brian said.

"Wait, are you sure? I thought I was Ryan," Ryan said.

"Let me think about that for a minute." Brian held his index finger near his chin and pursed his lips. "Oh, yeah, you're right. You are Ryan." The twins laughed.

"You're lucky I really want this coffee, or it would end up on both of you!" Amanda raised her middle finger and stalked off to the villa while the twins continued laughing.

When Brian arrived at the villa, Kira was waiting for him and was visibly upset.

"I thought this was supposed to be our honeymoon."

"Well, you were asleep. I didn't want to wake you, and Ryan and I usually meet in the mornings to run or work out. Now that you're awake, I can spend time with you." Brian hugged Kira and gave her a kiss.

"Well, our spa appointments start in an hour. We need to get there early, and it will take about twenty minutes to drive to the resort with the spa."

"How long will we be at the spa?"

"About four or five hours. Our first appointment is a couple's body scrub. We also have a massage, facial, and some type of mud bath scheduled," Kira said as she grabbed Brian's hand and pulled him toward the door.

Brian glanced at his watch. "Maybe we can meet with Ryan and Amanda for lunch."

Kira sighed. "Our spa package includes lunch. Remember? This is our day to just spend time with each other. After all, it is our honeymoon. I don't mind having Ryan and Amanda here as long as we get some alone time."

"You're right. It is our honeymoon, and I've just been acting like it's just a family vacation. So, here's what I'm going to do." Brian wrapped his arms around Kira and kissed her lips. "I promise to spend the rest of our honeymoon with you and only you."

"Why am I not completely convinced?"

"Okay, I'm gonna call my brother right now and tell him." After speaking with Ryan, Brian kept his promise to Kira and spent the rest of the honeymoon with only her.

FIVE

One month later, Brian and Kira settled into their life as a newly married couple. Kira had returned to work as a fourth-grade teacher after taking an extra week off for the honeymoon. She arrived home from work one afternoon and started cooking dinner. Brian entered the home carrying several bags filled with boxes. Kira glanced over at Brian.

"What did you do, go on a shopping spree?" Kira exclaimed as she stirred vegetables and chicken in a skillet.

"I just got some things for protection."

Kira gasped. "You bought a gun?"

"No." Brian chuckled. "Nothing like that. Let's see." Brian removed a large box out of one of his bags. "I have some security cameras."

"That looks like a lot of cameras."

"I have even more in the car. There's one for every room plus some for outdoors."

"Please say you're kidding," Kira scoffed. "Why in the world would we need so many security cameras? I certainly don't want one in every single room. You need to take those back!"

"They're for our own protection. Not only—"

"Haven't you heard about hackers? They can hack security cameras and see into your home."

"There are ways to protect against that. I plan to use very secure passwords. Also, Ryan helped me pick out a router that encrypts everything."

"Well, maybe keep them out of the bedrooms and bathrooms."

"Okay, that won't be a problem." Brian gathered the cameras and walked out of the kitchen.

"Where are you going? Dinner's almost ready."

"I was going to set some of these up, but I guess I can wait. I'm going to get the rest out of the car. I also bought one of those video doorbells." Brian took the security cameras and set them down onto a table in the family room. Then, he made two trips out to his car, returning each time with several boxes. Kira traipsed to the family room and perused the pile of boxes.

"Let's eat." Kira grabbed a plate of food and sat at the kitchen table.

Brian also got a plate and put food on it. He plopped down at the table across from Kira.

"So, what's going on?"

Brian shrugged his shoulders. "Nothing."

"There must be something going on. You bought a fancy alarm system and a pile of security cameras. Is there something I should know? Is someone after you? Are you suffering from paranoia? What is it?"

"No, none of that. I just want to make sure nothing happens. It's just precautionary."

"I know we discussed getting an alarm system, but all those cameras seem a bit much," Kira said.

"I think it might be fun to have a housewarming party next week."

"Is that why you bought all those cameras?"

"What? No!" Brian chuckled.

"Maybe a housewarming will be good in a couple of weeks. I'm getting my hair braided this Saturday and doing it two weeks from now will give me more time to get everything together."

After dinner, Kira went upstairs to get ready for bed while Brian installed and set up the security cameras and alarm system. After two hours passed, he yanked his cell phone out of his pocket and dialed Ryan's number.

"Hey, Brian. What's up?"

"Not much. I bought the security cameras for the

house. I will email the login information to you tonight. Check it out and let me know if you have any problems accessing the site or seeing the videos."

"Are they in every room?"

"No. Kira didn't want them in the bedrooms or bathrooms, so I agreed to not put them there."

"That's not right! I have them in every room in my house. You know I will need to know everything to have a successful switch day. We need to do as much as possible to avoid mistakes," Ryan said.

"Don't worry, I'll figure something out. Maybe I will just continue with the note-taking for everything that is said in those rooms. I don't think you really need to see or hear every single thing anyway. Maybe I will get some small digital recorders."

"Okay, that might work. I just want to make sure I know details about your conversations so she won't suspect something when I'm you."

"Kira and I are planning on having a house-warming party in two weeks. It will probably be on a Saturday. Do you think you and Amanda will be able to attend?"

"I can definitely attend, but I will have to check with Amanda."

"Man, when was the last time you saw her?" Brian chuckled.

"I don't even know. She left for China soon after we came home from our trip."

Brian looked up thinking he heard Kira coming down the stairs, but he was mistaken. "Well, hopefully she'll be back by then. Hey, man, I'm going to get off this phone. We'll talk more when I see you tomorrow morning."

"Okay, bye."

Brian trudged up the stairs and sauntered into the bedroom.

Kira exited the bathroom and sat on the bed. "Did you finish setting up the security system?"

"Not yet. I'll probably finish a little later this evening or before I hit the gym in the morning."

"You have plenty of time to do that. Let's go to bed."

Two weeks later, Brian and Kira got everything ready for their housewarming party. Brian picked up party platters from a local grocery store, and Kira cooked some of Brian's favorite soul food meals, including fried chicken, collard greens, and macaroni and cheese. Ryan and Amanda were the first to arrive. Other guests included Kira's friends and co-workers Karen and Elizabeth, Ryan and Brian's co-workers Sharon, James, and Eric, and Ryan and Brian's mother. After giving their guests a tour of their home, Kira and Brian invited everyone to eat dinner. Afterward, Brian invited everyone to play a guessing game.

"Hey, everyone. Ryan and I have a game for you. We will go upstairs and change into the same outfit. Then, you will have to guess which one is Ryan and which one is me. You'll need to write down your answer. Everyone who guesses the correct answer wins a prize."

Kira laughed. "Oh, I know my husband. This should be easy."

"Don't be too sure." Ryan handed out a piece of paper and pen to everyone.

"Well, that's not fair. I barely know you guys. I can't tell the difference between you two with how you're dressed now," Karen exclaimed as she yanked the piece of paper and pen out of Ryan's hands.

"Everyone will ask questions and examine us, but note, we will not remove any clothing for your examination. Also, you have five minutes to take a close look at us, before we change clothes." Brian scanned the room to see if everyone seemed ready with a pen and paper in hand.

"I'll just see what Kira and Amanda write because they should know which one is their husband." Sharon laughed as she tossed her flaming red hair.

"You shouldn't allow your wives or your mother to enter the contest," Karen said as she chugged some wine. "That's not fair."

Brian raised his arm and peeked at his watch. "Everyone can enter the contest and your five minutes start now!" Brian and Ryan stood next to each other.

Amanda stood and walked over to the twins. "Okay, can both of you turn around in a circle?" Brian and Ryan slowly turned around three times. "Wow, I never realized how much you two look alike. I guess I spend way too much time away from home."

"Can you stand back-to-back?" Elizabeth walked and stood several inches from the twins, looking at them as she wrote notes on her piece of paper.

"Ryan was always a little taller," said the twins' mother.

"Well, it looks like they're the same height now! I can't even see a weight difference," Karen exclaimed.

Kira stood in front of Ryan and Brian and examined them. "Hold your arms out in front and stand shoulder to shoulder."

"Do you have any tattoos?" Karen inquired.

"No tattoos. Okay, everyone, time's up, so we will go get changed. When we return, we will have a letter pinned to our shirts, and you will need to guess who we are. Everyone who gets the correct answer will receive a twenty-five-dollar gift card from their favorite restaurant." Brian and Ryan left the room and went upstairs to change their clothes.

Elizabeth sat down next to Kira. "Kira, what do you think?"

"Well, I knew which one was my husband when they were standing here."

"I mean what are some of their differences?"

"You know, I never really thought about that too much. I never see them wearing the same outfit, so I always know which one is Brian."

After fifteen minutes, Brian and Ryan returned. Both wore red sweatshirts, blue jeans, blue socks, and black gym shoes. Brian had the letter 'A' pinned to his sweatshirt while Ryan had the letter 'B' pinned to his sweatshirt.

"On your piece of paper, write our names and whichever letter you believe we're wearing. Don't forget to write your name at the top of the page. You may not ask any questions at this time," Ryan instructed.

"Kira, what are you gonna put?" Karen tried to peek at Kira's paper, but Kira blocked Karen's view with her arm.

After writing on her paper, Amanda folded it and handed it to Ryan. "I just guessed. So, whichever one of you is my husband, please don't be mad if I get this wrong."

"Momma Wright, which one is Ryan?" Karen tried to sneak a peek at Margaret's paper.

"I used to be good at telling them apart most of the time. Ryan used to be a little taller. Now, I'm not sure. I guess I'm like Amanda. I have to guess. Maybe, I'll just do eenie meenie miney mo." Margaret snickered.

"Is anyone confident about the answer?" James crumpled up his paper and tossed it toward Ryan and Brian. Ryan reached his right hand up and caught the paper. No one said anything. Gradually, everyone else handed in their answers to Ryan and Brian.

"Now that everyone has submitted their answers, we will identify ourselves. Ryan is standing next to me with the letter 'B,' so that means I am Brian with the letter 'A.' We will review your answers and announce the winners shortly." Ryan and Brian walked to a nearby table and separated the papers into correct and incorrect piles. After separating the papers, Brian picked up the correct forms.

"Okay, everyone, we have the winners. Winners, let me know the name of your favorite restaurant so we can order your gift cards. And now, the winners are Amanda, Sharon, and Elizabeth."

Kira immediately stood up. "Are you serious? Are you seriously saying I don't know my own husband? I don't believe it. This has to be a trick. I want a recount." Kira thought about the implications of not being able to recognize her husband. Would she make the same mistake Amanda had made at the wedding? She certainly didn't want to accidently kiss someone else's husband. There were a few times when Brian said something odd, and she wondered if she was really speaking to Brian, but she trusted him. She knew in her heart that he would never deceive her...or would he?

Margaret put her arm around Kira. "Oh, don't worry, honey. I got it wrong too, and I've known them their entire lives. It was just a game. Don't take it too seriously."

Six

B rian and Ryan were alone in the gym locker room the morning after the housewarming party.

"It was pretty funny how most of them couldn't tell us apart. We are too good." Ryan laughed.

"Yeah, well, don't get too comfortable. We have to keep our game up. The minute we become overly confident, mistakes happen."

"So, did you weigh yourself today?" Ryan opened a locker and shoved his bag into it.

"Yeah, 196."

"Oh, I'm 194."

"Well, you better gain two pounds." Brian chuckled.

"There might be some water weight. Let's get our workout on and weigh ourselves afterwards."

"I don't think anyone will notice a two-pound difference."

"We don't want to take any chances." Ryan picked up his small towel off the bench and jumped up. "Let's go get our workout on!"

"Okay. It's my turn to lead. We'll start on the treadmill for thirty minutes, then stretch, and finish up with weights and a final stretch." Brian got up off the bench, and both men left the locker room.

After working out, Brian and Ryan headed back to the locker room.

"Here are my notes for the last twenty-four hours. Did you get a chance to look at any of the security camera footage?" Brian fished a small notepad out of his over-stuffed duffle bag and handed it to Ryan.

"I looked at some. To save time, let's exchange notes about important conversations and when they occurred. We can scan the footage and look at the important parts if we need more info. Otherwise, we'll be staring at footage most of the day and all night. I certainly don't have time for that." Ryan chuckled. "Did you look at any footage from my home?"

"Bro, I tried, but I fell asleep after a few minutes." Brian laughed. "I agree though. We need to come up with a better system. It sounded like a cool idea when we planned it, but now, I don't know."

"Okay, I'll think about things and see if I can come up with something better."

"Cool. We're switching today, right? Is there anything I definitely need to know?" Brian asked.

"No. Amanda leaves for another business trip this evening. She might be gone by the time you get there. If not, she'll be on her way out."

"Well, Kira is still upset about losing that contest yesterday. She couldn't figure out how she could not recognize me. Then, she grilled me, asking a million questions about how we're different. I laughed and told her we weren't different and that we were in fact the same person. She really got mad then." Brian chuckled. "I told her I can prove we're the same person. All we have to do is take a DNA test. She stormed out of the room and slammed the door shut."

"Man, you need to stop teasing her like that. Maybe we need to choose a different day to switch things up. If she's that upset, it might be better for you to deal with it."

"I am dealing with it. I'm dealing with it through you!"

"You always get the easy way..." Ryan's phone rang, and he glanced at it. "Oh, wait, I need to take this." Ryan answered his phone as he quickly exited the locker room. Five minutes later, he returned.

"So, who was on the phone?"

"Oh, no one important. Just someone about a car."

"Customers are always important. I'm surprised they're calling this early."

Ryan stood and grabbed his duffle bag. "So, what do you say, switch places tomorrow instead of today so you can clear things up with Kira?"

"I trust you will do an excellent job clearing things up with Kira," Brian said. "And if you don't, don't worry. I have a very comfortable couch. You'll think you're sleeping on a cloud."

"Maybe this would be a good time for the two of us to go camping. It will give the wives time to cool off."

"Wives? Is something going on between you and Amanda?"

"She's been talking about going to some sort of counselor. She's not even here. I don't even remember what country she's in. I guess she plans on doing some sort of teleconference. I personally think we can work through things ourselves. We don't need a counselor."

"Well, I really love Kira, but sometimes..." Brian grabbed a hand towel from his bag and quickly wiped the sweat off his neck and face. "Anyway, I'm sure you and Amanda will work things out. You always do."

"Wait, what were you about to say? Sometimes what?"

"Nothin', man. You know Kira and I have the perfect relationship." Brian chuckled. "But even perfect relationships are not perfect, if you know what I mean. We have our disagreements. Sometimes, it's nice to get away for a little while, especially since your wife is AWOL. The alone time is nice."

"If you want, I'll give you all the alone time you want while I keep Kira entertained," Ryan said as he flexed while looking in the mirror.

"You better be joking!" Brian chuckled. "You are joking, right? Maybe I need to rethink this twin switching places thing and keep you away from my wife."

"Hey, if you can't trust me, who can you trust? Let's get out of here before we're late for work."

SEVEN

SEVEN YEARS LATER – BRIAN'S SHOOTING

Ryan had spent the entire night driving around his neighborhood searching for Brian. After returning home, he sat at the kitchen table and sluggishly slurped cereal, trying to gain an ounce of energy. Every few minutes, he pried his heavy eyelids open as he shoved the spoon into his mouth. Kira sauntered into the kitchen and brewed some coffee. She had no idea that Brian and Ryan had switched places and that Ryan was posing as Brian.

"I don't even feel safe in this town anymore," Ryan confessed to Kira as he yawned. "I keep dialing his number, expecting him to answer."

Kira glanced at Ryan. She barely recognized him.

He was disheveled, which made him look as if he had aged ten years overnight. "Well, I talked to Amanda for a few hours last night. She's going to get home as soon as possible. I also left a message for a friend who works in a hospital about a mile from Ryan's home. I want to have her check to see if he's there. Also, I'm getting ready to call some other hospitals in the area."

"We should go into hiding." Ryan stood up and paced before pouring a cup of coffee.

Kira sighed. "What?"

"Let's leave the house and hide somewhere. Someone might be after me."

"What? Where's this coming from?" Kira crinkled her eyebrows. His behavior shocked her. She never saw any signs of fear in her husband before. "You're just tired. You need to get some rest before—"

"Look at what happened to my brother." Ryan pounded his fists on the table, and the veins in his neck began to bulge. "In fact, Amanda and Olivia should move too. Whoever did something to Ryan knows where he lives. What if Amanda and Olivia are in danger? What if someone goes after them too?"

"We don't know what happened to him. Besides, we have so many security cameras, and they're monitored. Someone will see something if it happens."

"My brother also owned security cameras with monitoring."

"We need to be rational. Wait." She paused. "Is there something I should know? Were you and Ryan involved in something? If our family is in danger, I need you to tell me now."

"We're identical. What if they come after me too?"

"They? They who? Who are you talking about? Did someone threaten the two of you?" As an only child, Kira could not fully understand the relationship between her husband and his brother. Sometimes, she felt as if they were completely addicted to each other's presence.

"No, I just... I don't know. I don't know how to even live without him."

"We'll get through this together." Kira gently placed her hand on Ryan's shoulder.

Ryan stood up and walked toward the outside door.

"Where are you going?"

A warm tear drop rolled down Ryan's cheek, and his vision blurred. "I just need to clear my head. I just need to think about something."

"Brian, let's talk about this."

"I'll be back." Ryan headed toward the door.

"Wait, before you go, why don't you call Amanda?"

"Later." Flustered, Ryan quickly left out the door and slammed it shut.

Kira and Brian's six-year-old daughter, Jessica, walked into the kitchen. "Mommy, where's Daddy?"

"I don't know, sweetie. He went for a walk. What's wrong?"

"Have you seen my book bag?"

"No, I'll go look for it. Did your father feed you breakfast?"

"No. I'm hungry," Jessica whined.

"Okay, let me get you some cereal, and then, I'll look for your bag." Kira yawned as she poured some cereal for Jessica and walked around the house searching for Jessica's book bag. Kira's phone rang, and the caller ID showed Amanda's name.

"Hey, Amanda."

"Hi, Kira. I have a huge favor. I'm at the airport, and I don't know if I will be able to make it home before the end of the day." Amanda sniffled several times. "Anyway, I received a crazy call from the nanny. She suddenly quit, and she wants to know where to take the baby."

"Oh my God!"

"Can she drop Olivia off with you until I can get home? This whole thing is insane. First Ryan, now this!"

"Um, okay. Well, I'll have to work on getting a substitute for my class, but sure, I can watch her. Actually, I can just go pick her up from the nanny as soon as I put in for the sub."

"Okay, great! You're a lifesaver! I'm doing everything to get home as soon as possible." Amanda could be heard blowing her nose. "As soon as I get in, I will head straight to your home."

"Hey, don't worry about it. I look forward to spending time with Olivia."

"Okay, thanks again. By the way, any news about Ryan?" Amanda asked.

"No, not yet."

"Okay, they're calling me. Gotta go."

"Okay, bye." Kira hung up the phone and walked around the entire house looking for Jessica's bag. Finally, she located it in the basement at the bottom of the stairs. After jogging back up the stairs, she hurried into the kitchen and set the bag on the floor next to Jessica.

"Hurry, Jess. The bus will be here soon." Kira grabbed Jessica's bag and opened it. "Did you put your homework in here?"

"Yeah."

Kira continued flipping through the bag's contents. "I don't see it. Are you sure it's in here?"

"Oh, um, maybe. Oh, I know. It's on my desk."

"Okay. Go grab your homework and hurry."

Jessica jumped up from the table and dashed away to get her homework. Ryan entered the kitchen through the outside door.

"The bus is here." Ryan grabbed a mug from the cabinet and poured coffee into it from the coffeepot. Then, he plopped down at the table.

"Okay. Jess, it's time to go. The bus is here," Kira yelled.

Jessica scampered into the kitchen holding several pieces of paper. Kira picked up the book bag and handed it to her. After stuffing the paper into her bag, Jessica ran out the door.

"Can you believe her? She forgot to give me a kiss goodbye."

"The bus was here." Ryan sighed and stared blankly.

"Yeah." Kira noticed tears rolling down Ryan's cheeks. She grabbed a napkin from the counter and gently dabbed the corners of his eyes. "Stay home today."

"I have meetings." Ryan took a sip of coffee. "Something weird happened."

"What?"

"When I was out, something weird happened. I was walking, and a car driving down the street suddenly stopped. The driver rolled down the window and just stared at me."

"Do you think that may have something to do with your brother?"

Ryan sighed. "I don't know. I can't even think straight."

"Maybe it was just a coincidence, but you should tell the police. What color was the car?"

"I don't know. Green, blue. It wasn't clear."

"Honey, think. What did the driver look like?"

Ryan put his hands over his eyes and shook his head as he lowered it onto his arms.

"Well, I'm taking the day off. Amanda called. The nanny quit. She's on her way home, but I'm going to pick Olivia up and watch her until Amanda gets in."

Ryan lifted his head. "Did she say why?"

"Why what?"

"Why she quit."

"Well, that's the weird thing. She has no idea why she quit. I don't think she gave any type of reason she was quitting. Are you sure you don't want to stay home today? I'm sure they'll understand if you need to reschedule the meetings. Just tell them you have a family emergency. Besides, what are you going to tell them about Ryan?"

"Huh?"

"What are you going to tell your co-workers about why Ryan isn't at work?"

"Oh, I don't know. I didn't even think about that. Maybe I will take the day off." Ryan sighed. "Yeah, that might be best."

The doorbell rang. Kira glanced at her cell phone to

check the doorbell camera and saw Anne standing outside with Olivia.

"Who is it?"

"The nanny with Olivia. That's strange. I told Amanda I would pick Olivia up." Kira walked to the front door and opened it. The nanny quickly turned and walked away.

"Hi, Olivia."

"Hi, Auntie Kira." Olivia gave Kira a hug.

"Are you hungry? Did you eat breakfast?"

"I ate pancakes."

"Ooh, that sounds yummy."

Ryan walked to the front door.

"Daddy!" Olivia ran to Ryan and hugged him.

Kira sneaked next to Ryan and whispered, "Just go along with it for now."

"Hey, Olivia, let's go see what fun toys Jess has in her bedroom." Ryan picked up Olivia.

"Yay!"

Eight

Two men removed Brian from the trunk, wrapped him up with a thin, black rug, and placed him in a large tractor trailer underneath a large rug in the trailer. They drove toward the Mexican border. One man, Al, was tall and slender with dark brown hair and green eyes, while the other man, Bob, was short and muscular with blond hair and blue eyes.

"Where we goin'?" Bob pulled out a cigarette and lit it.

"Mexico. We got some guys down there who are good at getting rid of things."

"You don't think there will be problems at the border?"

"Nope. We got some guys at the border too. No worries there. No worries at all." Al rolled down his window two inches.

"And where do we go once we're down there?"

"You sure got a lot of questions. Just do what I tell you. That's all you need to know."

The men arrived at the border and breezed through inspection as predicted. After passing through the border, they drove two hours to a dump. They went to the back of the truck, unrolled the carpet, dragged Brian out of the truck, and then tossed him into a pile of garbage. Al grabbed the carpet and tossed it over Brian's body. Brian's head remained slightly uncovered.

"I know you said no questions, but it's my grandbaby's birthday. I'm hoping to make it back before too late."

"Okay, we're done. We're leaving the truck here and taking that blue car back."

"Yo, why are we..."

Al shot Bob a stern look.

"Never mind. Look, I'm an inquisitive guy. I like to know things."

There was a small, two-door, dark blue car parked fifty feet away. The two men walked to the car and drove back to the United States. Al dropped Bob off at his home and handed him an envelope filled with cash. Bob opened the car door. "Okay, Bob, you know what not to do."

"I know. I know. Don't say nothin' to nobody and don't ask no questions."

"Tell that grandbaby of yours happy birthday for me."

"You wanna come in and say it yourself?"

"No, I got things to do and trash to get rid of."

"Yo, do you know why... Oh, never mind." Bob walked away and went into his home.

NINE

THE NEXT MORNING

Kira and Ryan were in bed. It was early morning, and they had just woken up. Ryan perused information on his cell phone while Kira watched news on the television, both searching for any information that could lead them in the right direction.

"So, are you going in to work today?" Kira said as she flicked off the television.

"Yeah. I'm going to meet with everyone about my brother. I haven't decided what I'm going to say, but I need to have another salesperson take over his customers for now."

"Well, you really don't know what happened to him.

You may need to tell your co-workers what you know in case the police start asking them questions."

"Maybe I won't give them all the gory details. I'll just tell them he's missing."

"Are you sure you're going to feel like working?"

Ryan sighed. "Yeah. I'm just going to try to not think about it too much. After meeting with everyone, I plan to focus on work."

"I'm sure they'll understand if you just work a half day."

Kira's cell phone rang. She picked up the phone and saw that Amanda was calling.

"Good morning, Amanda."

"Hey, Kira. I am so sorry. My first flight was delayed. Then, I went on standby for another flight, but there wasn't enough room. I finally was able to get on a different flight, but it was delayed, and I missed the connection. Now, I'm waiting for another flight that doesn't leave until two hours from now. This whole thing has been an absolute nightmare!"

"Girl, don't even worry about it."

"I just want you to know I really am trying. I'm doing everything I can to get there. How's my baby?"

"She's doing well. She's asleep in Jessica's room on a cot. The girls really seemed to enjoy playing with each other. Oh, we didn't tell her anything about her father. She saw Brian and called him Daddy. We felt she might be too young to understand."

"Yeah, I'm sure I would have felt the same way. I do want to figure out a way to explain things to her, but I'm glad you didn't say anything. If things go as planned, I should be able to pick her up around noon. Any updates on Ryan?"

"Nothing yet."

"Oh, I hear my name. Gotta go. Bye!"

After hanging up with Amanda, Kira showered and got dressed.

"What are your plans for today?" Ryan climbed out of bed and walked toward the bathroom. His movements were unusually slow and robotic.

"Well, after Amanda picks Olivia up, I want to see if they discovered any clues about what happened to Ryan. I also want to see if there's any information you or I can provide that will assist with their investigation. I called off work for today." Kira looked at the man she believed to be her husband. She could sense that he was trying to be stoic while crumbling on the inside. She felt it was best for her to communicate with the police about their investigation.

Kira leaned over to pick up her phone off the night-stand, but the phone slipped out of her hand and fell underneath the bed. She got down on her hands and knees and looked under the bed. While picking up the phone,

Kira saw a small rectangular silver item under the bed. She lifted it up along with the phone.

"Brian, what's this?" Kira extended her arm toward Ryan with the silver item nestled in her hand.

Ryan quickly walked over to Kira and yanked it out of her hand. "Oh, that's nothing, really. It's just a recorder I use to take notes. For work. It must have slipped out of my pocket. I was wondering where it was."

"Well, I'm going to wake up the girls. Oh, before you leave for work, can you leave information for the detective who is investigating your brother's case?"

"Sure."

Later that afternoon, Amanda stopped by to pick up Olivia. As soon as Kira opened the front door, Olivia ran and jumped into Amanda's arms.

Amanda lifted Olivia up in the air. "Hey, honey, I missed you so much. Thank you so much for everything, Kira."

"Oh, no problem. I just can't believe what happened, but I'm going to meet with the detective today to see if there are any leads."

Amanda set Olivia down on the floor. "If you can wait until I freshen up and get a bite to eat, I can go with you."

"Don't worry about that. You go relax and spend time with Olivia. I will let you know what I find out."

"Okay, give me a call as soon as you leave the station. I

know I said this before but thank you so much!" Amanda leaned over and hugged Kira. "Olivia, let's go have some fun at Nana and Papa's house."

Kira walked into the police station and approached the reception desk.

"Hello, may I help you?"

"Yes." Kira pulled a business card out of her purse and glanced at it. "Is Detective Darren Grimes available?"

"Let me check." The reception clerk called Detective Grimes on the phone. "Detective Grimes, you have a visitor. Okay, I will let her know." The clerk hung up the phone. "Ma'am, he will be with you shortly."

"Thank you."

Ten minutes later, Detective Grimes exited the elevator and walked over to the reception clerk. The clerk pointed at Kira. Detective Grimes approached Kira.

"I'm Detective Grimes. How may I help you?"

"Hi, my name is Kira Wright. You spoke with my husband, Brian, about his brother who's missing."

"Walk with me to my desk." Detective Grimes and Kira got on the elevator and rode it to the third floor. "My desk is over to the left."

They walked to his desk and sat down.

"I remember speaking with your husband about his brother. How's he doing?" Detective Grimes looked at his computer screen to review the reports and notes about the case.

"He's trying hard to be strong, but I know it's difficult. That's why I'm here. I don't think he's in any condition to communicate with anyone right now."

"We really don't have any leads about what happened to your brother-in-law. I spoke with his wife and neighbors. There are no signs he had any enemies. We suspect a burglary gone wrong."

"I would have thought they would have stolen his crazy expensive car if they were going to steal something," Kira said.

Detective Grimes shrugged his shoulders. "Well, they may have been trying to get something quick and easy."

"If this was just a burglary, then where is Ryan?"

"That's a great question. Unfortunately, I don't know the answer. I do plan to speak with his co-workers and friends over the next couple of days. I also want to speak to your husband to see if he noticed any suspicious activity in the days before his brother's disappearance."

Kira sighed. "Do you believe there's still a chance he may be found alive?"

"We haven't found his body, so it's possible. It's very unusual for a crime to occur in his neighborhood. It has one of the lowest crime rates in the county, so we're really concerned."

"I want to do something, but I feel so helpless. I was going to put up missing person posters, but then I realized they might cause confusion since he has an identical twin brother. I don't know what to do."

"Don't worry. We are working hard on the case, and we investigate every tip that comes in on our tip line. I treat every missing person case as if I'm looking for my relative." Detective Grimes reached into his desk drawer and pulled out a brochure. "Here's some information about a support group for local families who are going through a difficult time. Perhaps some additional support can help your husband."

"Thank you, Detective," Kira said as she stood to leave. "And about those tips, you received some tips about him?"

The detective sighed. "Well, unfortunately most of the tips were from people who saw your husband and thought he was his missing brother. The identical twin element adds an additional layer of complication to cases like this."

"Right. Well, let me know when you find out something." As Kira walked away from Detective Grimes's office, she saw Olivia's nanny, Anne, standing near the exit talking to a very tall, skinny young man. As Kira approached the exit, Anne glanced in her direction. Kira smiled. "Anne?"

Anne nodded. After noticing Kira staring at the man who was with her, she said "Oh, um, this is my boyfriend, Tony."

"Hello, Tony. Nice to meet you. Anne, are you here to help with the investigation?"

Anne looked really confused. "Investigation?"

"The investigation to find out what happened to Ryan, your employer. Are you here to speak with the detective? His office is over—"

Tony grabbed Anne's arm, pulling her toward the door. "We gotta go," he said as he pushed the door open.

"Oh, okay. Well, it was nice meeting you and Anne, you take care." Kira left the building and drove home.

As Kira drove away, Tony walked down the street at a rapid pace while Anne struggled to keep up with him. "Um Tony, wait."

"I'm not doing this."

"We talked about this. What's up with you? Tony, please stop."

After walking two blocks, Tony slowed his pace. "Look, this wasn't part of the plan. You know I hate being around the police, and then, you want me to go to the police station with you?"

"It's just while I answer a few more questions about the security system. Then we can leave and never go back."

Tony stopped walking and faced Anne. "Are you really

that dumb? You don't think they're going to suspect you of something? The broken security system. Your missing boss. I don't even know why I agreed to this."

"But I need you for support. If we don't cooperate, they'll really start thinking something. They're gonna think we did something to Mister Wright."

Tony wrapped his arms around Anne. "Come away with me. We can go stay with my parents in Texas until we figure things out."

Anne sighed as she pulled away from him. "I'm going back to the station. I just need to do this. Don't worry. I won't tell them what you did to the security system."

"Well, I'm not going with you." Tony waved his hand and walked away.

Anne froze for several minutes after he left. She strolled back to the police station and watched people entering and leaving the station for fifteen minutes before turning around and going home.

Detective Grimes searched the database for suspects who'd been picked up within the last twenty-four hours and charged with various crimes. One man named Drew Ronstone caught his attention. Why did he seem so familiar? Detective Grimes dialed the arresting officer.

"Officer Wayman speaking."

"This is Detective Grimes. I'm investigating a case, and I saw that you arrested a Drew Ronstone."

"Oh, yes. We had an undercover sting on that one. We got some help from a guy at some luxury car dealership."

"His name wasn't Ryan Wright, was it?"

"No. Why do you ask?"

"Oh, it's not important. Hey, can you send over the full file on Ronstone? I'm wondering about something with a case I'm working on."

"Sure. Can you give me a couple of hours? I'm in the middle of picking someone up."

"No problem." After ending the call, Detective Grimes continued searching the database for clues before heading home.

Ten

Ryan sat for hours every day reviewing his copy of his home's security footage for the day Brian disappeared. Since he had access to the system from his current home, it was easy to view the saved videos. The more he viewed the footage, the more things did not make sense. The footage ended abruptly on the morning of Brian's disappearance as if a plug had been pulled. Also, it appeared that some of the footage may have been deleted. Ryan decided to visit Anne to see if she could provide any additional information about what happened to the security system.

After quitting her job as Olivia's nanny, Anne moved into a small one-bedroom apartment in a quaint, tree-lined neighborhood. Although Ryan was able to locate an address for her online, he wasn't sure if the address was accurate. Upon arriving at the apartment building, Ryan sat in his car for several minutes looking to see if there were any signs that Anne lived there. He finally noticed her vehicle parked near the front of the building. He got out of the car and knocked on her door.

After knocking several times, Ryan turned to leave when no one answered. Suddenly, the door swung open, and Anne stood with her mouth gaping open. "Um, you're back? Mister Wright?"

"Oh, no. I'm Brian, his twin brother."

"Oh, okay. Why are you here?"

"I'm sorry. Is this a bad time? Can we talk?"

Anne grimaced. "Um, I already told the police everything." Anne began to shut the door, but Ryan held out his arm, blocking it from closing shut.

"I know. I just have a couple of questions about something I saw on the security camera. Can I come in?"

Anne sighed. "I really don't think I can help."

"I promise I won't take too much of your time. I just have a couple of quick questions. If you don't know the answers, I understand."

Anne's eyes searched around Ryan as if she was concerned that the police were nearby before allowing him to enter her apartment.

Upon entering the small, dimly lit apartment, Ryan noticed a pair of men's shoes near the door. In many ways, the apartment reminded him of his college days as it was filled with mismatch furniture and the type of décor typically found in college dorms and student apartments. Ryan slid his shoes off before proceeding further.

Anne walked over to the living room area. "Um, let's sit over here."

"Okay. As I said, I won't take up too much of your time. I know you said the alarm didn't come on after you set it, so you assumed it was broken?"

"Right." Anne fiddled with her clothing as she spoke.

"But when I reviewed the security system, it appears to have lost power or somehow died early in the morning soon after my brother left the house. It's as if there was an abrupt disconnect before you left the house to take Olivia to the park, but you didn't notice a problem with the alarm until you returned?"

"Uh, yeah."

"Another thing that baffles me is the system's memory. I don't know, I'm not an alarm expert, but it seems as if something was deleted before you left. I mean the time stamp seems off. Can you think of anything that may have happened?" Ryan glanced at Anne and noticed that her skin seemed flush, and her eyes began to water.

Anne lowered her head and continued fiddling with her clothing. "I had no idea something bad would happen. My ex-boyfriend came over and asked about the alarm system. He looked at things, and that's when I found out there was a camera in every room. He told me he would disconnect the camera in some of the rooms, but nothing seemed to work after that."

"Why did he want to know about the alarm system?"

"Um, I don't know," Anne said shrugging her shoulders. "I just thought he was being overprotective. I'm so sorry about your brother. I didn't know something bad would happen on the same day."

"Did you tell any of this to the police?"

"Um, I just told them the alarm broke."

Ryan sighed. "So, they have no idea your boyfriend had tampered with the alarm?"

"No. I'm sorry. I really am. I had no idea." Anne yanked some tissue out of a box and wiped the tears streaming down her face.

"Anne, where is he? Where's your boyfriend?"

"Uh, I don't know. He blocked my calls. I think he might have left town." Anne stood and began walking toward the door.

"What's his name?"

"Um, I really don't want to get involved. Look, I gotta cut this short. I have an appointment."

"Please, can I at least get a name? I won't involve you."

"I'm sorry. Please leave." Anne walked over to the door and opened it. "Goodbye."

Ryan drew in a frustrated breath and exited the apartment. After leaving, he called Detective Grimes and informed him about what he discovered. The detective promised to contact Anne and investigate the matter further.

Eleven

At a dump site on the outskirts of Tijuana, plump raindrops pounded Brian's face. He opened his eyes for a brief second but quickly passed out. Two young boys carrying flashlights snuck into the dump site to search for useful things to take home. One boy stumbled over Brian's legs and fell. As he stood up, he placed his hand near Brian's head and screamed when he looked down and saw Brian's face.

"What's wrong?" the other boy asked, speaking in Spanish.

"A man! A man! A dead man!" The young boy breathed heavily as he pointed to Brian's head. The other boy tiptoed over to his brother and peeked down. "Aah, let's tell Mom." The boys ran screaming as they hurried home.

Sirens filled the air. An ambulance arrived at the dump site. Two men exited the ambulance carrying a stretcher. They approached Brian.

"Is he alive?"

"He looks stiff as a board, but let me see if he has a pulse." He squatted down and picked up Brian's wrist. "I don't feel... Oh, wait. There is a pulse. It's very faint."

"Hurry, let's get him out of here." The men lifted Brian carefully and set him onto the stretcher. They carried him into the ambulance and hooked him up to oxygen and monitoring machines. The high-pitched siren blared as they sped to the nearest hospital.

TWELVE

Amanda decided to take her mind off her missing husband by going to a nearby shopping mall the morning after she picked Olivia up from Kira and Brian's house. As Amanda fastened Olivia's booster seat, her phone rang. Amanda noticed a missed call and listened to the voicemail message.

"Hello, Amanda, this is Detective Grimes. Please give me a call right away. You should have received a page with my number." Amanda immediately called the detective.

"Grimes speaking."

"Hello, Detective Grimes. This is Amanda Wright returning your call."

"Hi, Amanda, how are you?"

"Well, I guess I'll know once you tell me why you're calling."

Detective Grimes sighed. "Well, I don't know how you will feel about this. We found a male body. A hiker found him ten miles from your residence. He seems to match your husband's physical appearance, but we need you or another relative to go to the morgue to identify him. Now, there is a chance the body is not your husband's, but we need to make sure."

"Oh god, I hope it's not him!" Amanda's mind raced as she envisioned herself viewing her husband on a cold metal slab. She also imagined viewing the dead body of an unknown man. Although she did not want to see her husband dead, seeing the dead body of a random unknown person seemed bad too. It had been over ten years since she had been to a funeral and, even then, she could not force herself to look directly at the corpse.

"If you can go there and take a look today, that would be great. The morgue closes at five."

Amanda hesitated. She wondered if she could have someone else view the body. "I have my daughter here, so I won't be able to go right away."

"Any time before they close is fine."

"Okay, thanks." After hanging up the call with the detective, Amanda turned to Olivia. "Hey, Olivia, I have to go somewhere. How would you like to hang out with Auntie Kira?"

Olivia pouted. "You have to work?"

"No, honey, I don't have to go to work this time. I have to go somewhere else."

"Can I go somewhere else too?"

"Not today." Amanda dialed Kira's phone number, and Kira answered the call. "Hi, Kira, I don't mean to bug you, but I have a huge favor to ask of you. Are you busy?"

"Well, you called at a good time. I'm on my lunch break. What do you need?"

"Can I drop Olivia off at the school with you for a little while? I will pick her up in about an hour."

"Sure. What's going on?"

Amanda glanced back at Olivia, slowly stepped outside of the car, and partially closed the car door. "The police found a body, and they want me to go to the morgue to identify it."

"Oh no. I'm so sorry."

"I don't know why, but I really feel like it's not him. Or maybe I really don't want to believe it's him. Either way, I need to take a look."

"Well, you can definitely bring Olivia here."

"Thank you so much, Kira! You're a lifesaver!" After Amanda dropped off Olivia at the school where Kira taught, she drove to the morgue. After checking in at the morgue, an employee guided Amanda to a small room. Upon entering the room, Amanda saw a body covered with a white sheet. The morgue employee walked over to the body and uncovered its head. Amanda took a deep breath as she glanced at the body and immediately felt a surge of relief. She turned to the morgue employee and said without hesitation, "That's not him."

After leaving the morgue and picking up Olivia, Amanda returned home and called family members, friends, and neighbors to arrange a search party later that evening. She also had her secretary print flyers. Half of the people canvassed Ryan and Amanda's neighborhood while the other half searched a nearby park for clues. After canvassing the neighborhood, Kira, Ryan, and Jessica headed to Ryan and Amanda's home to provide support and console each other. Amanda served everyone ice cream, and they gathered in the family room to discuss Kira's meeting with the detective and possible options for finding out what happened to Brian, whom most people believed was Ryan.

While everyone ate ice cream and chatted, Ryan heard heavy footsteps on the porch outside. "Shhh!" he whispered and lifted his index finger up to his mouth. "I think someone's outside. Run upstairs and lock yourselves in the master bedroom. Call 911."

Kira scrunched her eyebrows. "Are you sure? I didn't hear anything," she said.

"Yeah, I just heard it again," Ryan whispered. "Hurry!"

Amanda scooped up Olivia. Kira and Jessica quickly followed her upstairs.

Dread bubbled up in Ryan's throat; he ran to his office, where he kept a handgun locked in a safe. Thankfully, it was already loaded. He flicked off the safety and cocked it as he tiptoed to the main foyer and hid in the front closet to listen for more noise outside. He grabbed his cell phone and glanced at the security camera app. He could see a large, muscular man standing near the front door.

Ryan's heart pounded as he heard the doorknob turn. The door creaked open ominously. The man stepped into the foyer gingerly, closing the door behind him. Ryan was shocked to discover that he had forgotten to lock the front door. He held his breath and waited for the intruder to cross past the closet.

Ryan slid the closet door open and pressed his pistol against the man's back. "Don't move," Ryan barked as he knocked the man's pistol out of its holster. It slid across the hallway and struck the baseboard with a thud.

Before Ryan could react, the man whipped around and knocked his gun out of his hand. Ryan grabbed the man forcing him off-balance. As the intruder fell, he tackled Ryan in a split-second retaliation. Both men plummeted to the floor. Ryan's jaw slammed against the floor, but he ignored the pain and scrambled to regain his footing. His gun was much closer to them than the other man's, and the two men locked eyes as they dove for it in unison.

As the man reached for Ryan's gun, Ryan balled up his fist and slammed it on the man's hand. Crack. The bones on the back of the man's hands snapped. Enraged, he swung for Ryan's head, but the angle was awkward, and he narrowly missed. Ryan swiped his gun and cocked it, pointing at the man's chest. In a last-ditch effort to overpower him, the man lunged at him again.

You're not getting the best of me, Ryan thought as he pulled the trigger. Blood, hot and viscous, spattered his cheek.

It took everything he had not to empty the contents of his stomach then and there, but Ryan held himself together as he made his way to the master bedroom door. He could faintly hear labored breathing.

"It's me. Everything's okay. Just don't come out here," he said softly as he stood in front of the bedroom door. Suddenly, he heard the lock turn. The door swung open before he could stop it. Amanda and Kira stood in the doorway, craning their necks to look down the stairs. "You don't want to—" he started. Both women flashed him a dirty look and pushed past him. "I'm serious; don't go down there!"

He rushed to catch up to them. Two bloodcurdling

screams echoed throughout the house. "I told you not to go," he sighed. Sirens wailed, and soon Ryan heard heavy footsteps outside the front door as he stared at the blood-stained wall. *I'll need to hire a service first thing in the morning to get that filthy blood off the walls*, he thought grimly. The last thing he wanted was to keep a visual reminder about what happened. He briefly closed his eyes as he tried to erase the image from his mind. Even though the man had attacked him, Ryan still felt traumatized by taking the man's life.

Ryan hobbled to the door and opened it. Detective Grimes walked in and looked down at the body. Kira and Amanda ran upstairs to make sure that Olivia and Jessica stayed in the bedroom.

Detective Grimes approached Ryan. "So, we meet again," he said, looking down at the bloody corpse. "Can you tell me what happened here?"

"Yeah. This man broke into the house and attacked me. I fought back and shot him." Ryan crossed his arms and rubbed them with his hands nervously. His gaze remained toward the floor.

"Anything else?"

"No, not really. I mean, I heard him coming in, so I ran to get a gun, and I hid in the closet over there. I had sent my wife and sister-in-law and the kids upstairs to hide. I came out of the closet and the guy fought with me. I was able to grab the gun off the floor and shoot him."

"Okay. Do you know him, or have you ever seen him before?"

"No."

One of the officers approached Detective Grimes and whispered to him. He then handed the detective a black wallet. Detective Grimes reviewed the driver's license in the wallet. "Do you know someone by the name of Alex Thomasson?"

"That name doesn't sound familiar."

"Well, it's going to take a while for us to investigate the scene, so we're going to ask that you clear the property."

"Okay, I'll let everyone know." Ryan walked upstairs and entered the bedroom. "Okay, everyone, the detective wants us to leave. Amanda, do you want to come with me and Kira?"

"No, I think Olivia and I will just head over to my parents' house."

Ryan scooped Olivia up. "Let's take the kids out the side door." As Ryan buckled Olivia into her car seat in Amanda's car, he gently kissed her forehead. "Amanda, let me know if you need anything. I'll call someone to clean up the mess."

When Kira arrived home with Jessica and Ryan, Kira and Jessica walked upstairs and went to bed. Ryan immediately picked up his laptop and sat at the kitchen table. Then he pulled up the security camera monitors on the computer and stared at the screen all night.

The next morning, Detective Grimes phoned Ryan and requested to meet with him at the station to finalize the police report. After Ryan showered and dressed, he headed to the police station to meet with the detective. When Ryan first entered Grimes's office, the detective picked up a file off his desk and reviewed the report and photographs.

"Mister Wright, one of the reasons I wanted to meet with you today was to discuss how what happened to you last night may be related to your missing brother. Something happened to your brother, and it appears that the same person may be going after you and your family. Can you think of any reason why someone might want to harm your family?"

"No, I really can't."

"What about any disgruntled employees or customers? Has anything unusual happened recently?"

"Well, I did have a strange encounter with a customer. He was angry because I refused to allow him to test-drive a car without a license and proof of insurance."

"What was his name?"

"I don't remember, but I can have my assistant forward his information to you," Ryan said.

"Okay, that would be great. Anything else?"

"Um, I don't think so. Most of my customers are nice, and they seem happy with our service. Oh, did you talk to Anne about the alarm? Remember, I told you about her boyfriend disconnecting the alarm?"

"Yes, I followed up with both Anne and her boyfriend, Tony Ronstone. Tony had an alibi when your brother went missing. He was clocked in at work. We also checked with his employer who confirmed his alibi. Anyway, there are a couple of leads we're investigating concerning two other men who may have purchased vehicles from your dealership. Are you familiar with your customer Drew Ronstone?"

Ryan needed to remind himself that he was Brian, so he had to think about how much Brian would have known about individual customers. "Um, that name does sound familiar. Is he related to Tony?"

"I'm not sure. Their last name isn't common, so I asked if they were related. They denied any family relationship, but I really don't know if that's true."

"I believe I may have seen it on one of my brother's customer reports, but I don't deal with most customers personally. Do you believe Drew may have something to do with what happened?"

"Well, I'm not sure. We arrested Mr. Ronstone for money laundering, and he was in prison when everything happened to your family. In fact, he's still there, but he knows a lot of dangerous people."

"Ronstone. Oh, I think I do remember him. He seemed like a cool guy. I mean Ryan spoke about him as if he was cool. Sometimes, he told me about some of the more interesting customers."

"There's also another customer we're looking into. His name is Marco Kameron. He also had some bad luck with violence against his family. Now, I don't know if it's connected to what happened to your family, but we were wondering if the people who attacked his family are the same ones going after your family."

"That name sounds very familiar."

Detective Grimes tilted his head down and peered over the upper rim of his eyeglasses. "From the customer reports?"

"Yes, from customer reports."

"Well, if you think of anyone we should investigate, please let me know. Meanwhile, your family may want to stay out of your brother's house for a while. And get me a list of every customer from the dealership along with their contact information."

"Okay, I'll go through my customer lists this evening.

I'll call you with the names of everyone I think you should contact."

After Ryan left, a young officer entered Detective Grimes's office and tossed a folder onto the desk.

"It's the fingerprint report," the officer said.

"The Wright case?"

"Yeah."

Detective Grimes grabbed the folder and quickly flipped through the report. Most of the fingerprints on Ryan's Porsche belonged to Ryan's family, but there was one match to a nonfamily member. Detective Grimes immediately phoned Ryan.

"Mr. Wright, I know you just left, but I just got some new information. Do you know a man by the name of Tommie Parker?"

"Um, no, I don't think so." He paused for several seconds, trying to recall if he'd heard the name. "Oh, wait. I remember now. He's the guy I mentioned earlier who was angry because we didn't allow him to do a test drive. We ended up having security escort him out. Do you think he did something to my brother?"

"I don't know, but his fingerprints were on the Porsche. When he was at the dealership, did you see him go near your brother's car?"

"I didn't see him after he left. Uh, actually my brother

was the one who met with him. I didn't see him. Is he a suspect?"

"No one is a suspect yet. We're just continuing our investigation, and we need to find out why his fingerprints were on your brother's Porsche."

Thirteen

etective Grimes was determined to find out what happened to Ryan Wright. Nothing about his disappearance made sense. He called Tommie Parker in for questioning. Two hours later, Tommie arrived at the police station.

When Detective Grimes sauntered into the dimly lit interrogation room, Tommie was seated at a table staring blankly at the one-way mirror on the opposite wall. Detective Grimes tossed his notebook onto the table before sitting and read Tommie his Miranda rights. Tommie nodded as the detective recited the rights.

"Mr. Parker, tell me what you did with Ryan Wright," Detective Grimes said as he peered intensely at Tommie.

"Huh," Tommie said, furrowing his brow.

"Look, I'll make this super easy for you. You tell me

what happened to Ryan Wright, and you might not have to spend the rest of your life in prison," Detective Grimes said as he peeled open his notebook.

"I don't know what you're talkin' about."

"Well, let me refresh your memory. I know you put your grubby fingers on Ryan Wright's Porsche. Your fingerprints were all over it."

Tommie's eyes lit up. "Oh, the Porsche? I love Porsches." Tommie saw Detective Grimes give him an intense look. "Look, whoever told you I stole that Porsche is lying. And it's not against the law to touch a car in a public place. I know some things about the law. I didn't open the door. I didn't steal it." Tommie stood up before remembering that his wrist was handcuffed to the table.

"Sit down," Detective Grimes yelled. The intensity of Detective Grimes's voice shook the table and startled Tommie as he sat down. "Look, I don't care anything about the Porsche, and I certainly don't want to spend all day in this tiny room with you. We can both get out of here if you tell me what happened to Ryan Wright. That's all I care about. What happened? Did you kill him when you tried to steal his car?"

"I don't know what you talkin' about. You think I killed someone? Man, I want a lawyer. I have nothin' to say. You can't hold me here. I want to speak to my lawyer." Tommie lifted his handcuffed arm and shook it. "As many times as I been here, you know I never killed no one. I ain't a murderer," Tommie huffed.

Detective Grimes leaned forward. "Okay, so let's say you didn't kill him. What did you do to him? Where is he?"

"I-want-my-lawyer! Plead the fifth. Plead the fifth."

Another detective opened the door and motioned for Detective Grimes. Detective Grimes sighed as he stood and left the room.

"Sir, I'm sorry to interrupt, but some important information came in on the Wright case. The chief wants to speak with you. If you want, I can finish up here and place a call in to his lawyer."

"Thanks. Did he say what he wanted?"

"No, sir."

Detective Grimes briskly headed toward the chief's office. When he entered, there were two other men and one woman seated in front of the chief's desk.

"Detective Grimes, grab a seat. This is Agent Woods, Agent Brown, and Detective Moore," the chief said.

As Detective Grimes pulled up a seat, the chief continued speaking and slid a manila folder toward the detective. "Since you're over the Ryan Wright case, I wanted you to sit in on this meeting. Grimes, have you come across the name Drew Ronstone during your investigation?"

"Actually, he was the next person I planned to interrogate," Detective Grimes said as he leaned forward, grabbed the folder, and perused its contents.

"Well, there was an undercover sting involving Ronstone. We also learned that the FBI was investigating Ronstone due to his multistate activities. Anyway, the FBI saw your guy, Ryan Wright, leaving Ronstone's facility several days before he disappeared."

Detective Grimes closed the folder. "Ronstone is a known customer of the dealership where Wright works. He's at the top of my list of people to interrogate. I've had my suspicions about him, but I wasn't sure if there was a deep connection between him and Wright."

"Well, a source informed the department that Ronstone may have targeted him believing that he was undercover or a police informant."

"I see. Well, I can head over there now to interrogate him."

"Don't forget the file and let me know immediately if you learn anything new." The chief stood, handed Detective Grimes the file folder, and escorted him to the door.

As Detective Grimes walked down the long, narrow hallway to the interrogation room, he perused the folder's contents. Was it possible that Ryan Wright became involved with a known felon with a mile-long rap sheet?

Things just didn't add up, but Detective Grimes was determined to find some answers.

Soon after Detective Grimes entered the cold interrogation room, an officer escorted a handcuffed Drew Ronstone into the room. Drew had a smug look on his face as he sat at the table across from Detective Grimes.

"Ronstone?"

Drew looked at the detective and shot him a venomous look that pierced the detective's soul. Detective Grimes straightened his body and shifted in his chair slightly. "Okay, I'm going to cut to the chase. I don't want to waste your time, and I certainly don't want you wasting mine. So, tell me, where is Ryan Wright? We know he was in contact with you about a car."

"I already told them. I have nothing more to say."

Detective Grimes leaned forward. "You were one of the last people to see him. I know you met with him about a car. What happened after that?"

"I-don't-know. He left my garage. That's it. Nothing else happened. I already told all this to that other guy."

"Okay, so maybe you don't know, but I bet you know someone who does. Which one of your associates should I speak to next?"

"Oh, I don't know. Maybe Mother Teresa?" Drew leaned far back in his chair and closed his eyes.

"You know how these things work. You help me, and maybe I can help you too."

"That's what they always say. You can't come up with something original?"

"Well, maybe you'll be ready to talk when you get tired of spending so much time behind bars." Detective Grimes stood and exited the room. He was beyond frustrated and hoped to have some answers for Ryan Wright's family. No matter what happened, he was determined to find out what happened to Ryan Wright. It was late, so he decided to go home and return the following morning with a fresh pair of eyes.

Fourteen

MEXICAN HOSPITAL

Brian lay motionless in a hospital bed. Dr. Rodriguez stood by Brian's bedside speaking to a nurse, Paulina, who had just arrived for her shift. Dr. Rodriguez was a tall, slender man with a large mustache that seemed to take over half of his face. He stared at his notes on the computer as he spoke.

"This man arrived as a John Doe with a gunshot wound to his chest and a wound from blunt force trauma to the head. They found him with no ID, and he doesn't appear to be a local resident. Well, none of the staff around here recognizes him, and they know everyone. We were able to remove the bullet during surgery. Now, we have him in a medically induced coma until he stabilizes."

"What's the prognosis?" Nurse Paulina asked.

"It's too soon to tell. He was unresponsive when he arrived, and we won't know if there is any brain damage until we take him out of the coma. He's a very lucky man. The bullet just missed his artery by about four to six centimeters, and his bleeding seemed to be minimized due to compression. Something must have been pressing down on him to slow down the bleeding. This colder than usual weather pattern probably helped some too."

"How long do you expect to keep him in the coma?"

"It's too soon to tell. I estimate two weeks to a month."

Another nurse entered the room. "Doctor, those CT scan results you asked about came back."

"Thanks, Ana. Excuse me, I need to look at those results. Look at my notes and let me know if you have any questions." The doctor left the room.

Ana walked over to Brian's bed and peered at him. "What's his story?"

"Oh, I don't know much. He's in a medically induced coma," Paulina said.

"That's a nasty gash on his head. He's a good-looking man, even with that nasty gash."

Paulina shrugged her shoulders. "I didn't even think about that."

"Well, let me know when he wakes up. I want to meet him."

"*Chica*, get out of here!" Paulina waved her hand, shooing Ana away.

FIVE WEEKS LATER

Nurse Paulina checked Brian's vitals. Dr. Rodriguez walked into the room, pushing a computer cart with a laptop sitting on top of it. He logged onto the computer and reviewed Brian's chart.

"Looks like he's ready. Time to take him out of the coma today. I put the order in his chart to reduce the anesthetics."

"Okay, I will take care of that now." Nurse Paulina reviewed the information on the computer and replaced his IV fluids.

"Also, let me know when he wakes up. We'll want to let the police know so they can question him about what happened. They believe he might be American or from another country."

Two hours later, Brian opened his eyes. Hospital machinery beeped distantly in his ears. For a moment, he couldn't register pain, or the despair of the situation, just a sense of comfort and calm. He felt warm and safe under the thick blanket, content to think of nothing. He seemed to be at peace; then, in an instant, he felt a sharp stabbing pain in his head. He grimaced. Nurse Maria walked into Brian's room to check his vitals.

"Welcome back. I'll go get the doctor," Nurse Maria said in Spanish as she pivoted and left the room. Five minutes later, she returned with Dr. Rodriguez.

Dr. Rodriguez walked to Brian's bedside and checked his pulse. Speaking in Spanish, the doctor greeted Brian. "Hello, sir. Can you tell me your name?"

Brian looked confused. "Um..."

Dr. Rodriguez changed the tone of his voice. "What's your name? Do you know your name?"

Brian tried to think about what his name might be. The more he tried to think, the more his head ached. He closed his eyes. "No. I don't know." Although Brian studied Spanish in college and remembered basic conversational Spanish words, he answered the doctor's questions in English.

"Do you know where you are?"

Brian peeled his eyes open and turned his head slightly as he glanced at the doctor. "No."

"You are in a hospital. You have a head injury. You also suffered a gunshot wound in your chest. Do you know what year this is?"

"Um, nineteen, uh, twenty... I'm not sure."

Realizing that Brian seemed to be fluent in English,

Dr. Rodriguez switched to communicating with him in English. "Do you remember anything about what happened to you?"

Brian shook his head.

"Can you move your leg?"

Brian gently shook his right leg.

"Can you raise your arm?"

Brian raised his right arm a few inches off the bed.

"Okay, I'll let you get some rest. Maria, I'm going to order psych and physical therapy for him. Let Paulina know when she comes back from break."

Three hours later, the psychologist came to meet with Brian. After meeting with Brian and asking him questions, she diagnosed him with retrograde amnesia.

"Doctor, will I ever regain my memory?"

The psychologist sighed. "You may start to remember bits and pieces of your memory over time. It's too soon to know how much of it you will regain, but there are steps you can take to try and get your memory back. The good news is that you can communicate well and control your body, so there doesn't seem to be any major brain damage."

Nurse Paulina entered Brian's room. "Well, hello there. It's good to see you decided to join us in the land of the awaken."

Brian squinted his eyes from the bright lights and

glanced at Paulina. "They said I have amnesia." The idea of never knowing who he was terrified Brian to the core. "Do you think you can get me a hand mirror so I can see my face?"

"Of course." Paulina left the room and returned with a small mirror and handed it to Brian. He gazed in the mirror, but even his face seemed foreign and unfamiliar. He didn't remember seeing that face before. Brian strained his brain trying to obtain a glimmer of his past life. Who was he? Where was he from? And, more importantly, what had he done to get shot? Even without a memory, he did not feel as if he were the type of person who would be involved in a life of crime.

Two hours later, two police officers showed up to question Brian. They had waited weeks to interview the John Doe with a bullet hole. Even after questioning the children who found him and residents who lived near the dump site, they still had no clues. They suspected that he was not local to the area, but they were not sure if he was American or from another part of Mexico. There was no record of someone traveling to Mexico matching Brian's description. They hoped that interviewing him would provide answers.

When the officers entered Brian's room, one stood on the right side of Brian's bed while the other one stood on the left side. Both officers carried small notepads. The one who stood on Brian's right side spoke first.

"Hello, my name is Officer Vasquez, and this is my partner, Officer Ramos. Tell me, what's your story?"

Brian turned his head toward Officer Vasquez and tried to widen his half-closed eyes as he cleared his throat. "I was hoping you could tell me something. The doctor said I have amnesia."

Officer Vasquez leaned over, placing his hands onto Brian's bed. "Amnesia, huh? Do you really think I was born yesterday? What were you involved in that got you shot? I will find out, so don't waste your time lying to me."

"I'm not lying. Ask my doctor."

"No passport or ID were with your belongings. You're obviously not from around here. How did you get into this country? Who snuck you in?" Officer Vasquez lifted his notepad and held his pen, prepared to write.

"I don't know."

The tone of Officer Vasquez's voice grew in intensity. "Don't lie to me! If you don't tell me the truth, I will arrest you. As soon as you get out of this hospital, you're going nowhere but jail."

Brian sighed. "I really don't know. They told me I was found in a dump. I was shot."

Officer Ramos spoke up. "Who shot you?"

"Don't know," Brian said as he slowly shrugged his shoulders. "I don't remember anything."

Officer Vasquez increased the pressure of his hands on

Brian's bed, causing the sheets to tighten around Brian. "The bigger question is how did you get into Mexico? We combed through images of everyone crossing our borders. There were no records of you coming here. Just tell us the truth. We'll bring in a lie detector test, so you better just tell us the truth now."

Brian felt his blood pressure increasing by the minute. Monitors attached to Brian's body started beeping rapidly. Nurse Paulina entered the room.

"Excuse me, officers, you'll need to leave now. This patient needs his rest."

Officer Vasquez handed Nurse Paulina a card. "Call me as soon as he's discharged." Then he turned to Brian and placed a card on his bedside table. "I'm leaving this for you. Come down to the station when you leave. We're not done questioning you."

Fifteen

One week after the intruder entered her home, Amanda returned home to inspect it for any signs of blood or other residue from the shooting. As she stepped into the house, lemon-scented cleanser stung her nostrils. She quickly picked Olivia up and walked around the home checking the walls and flooring. After being satisfied that the home had been thoroughly cleaned, she set Olivia down and plopped down onto the sofa. She still wasn't comfortable sleeping at the house. The thought of being home alone after the intrusion scared her, and she wasn't sure that she would ever be able to sleep here. For the time being, she spent most of the day at her home and spent nights at her parents' house. This was Amanda's new normal until she was sent to the next destination for work.

A few hours later, Kira arrived and rang the doorbell.

Two minutes later, Amanda opened the front door with Olivia skipping along right behind her.

"Hey, Amanda. How are you?" Kira looked down and noticed Olivia. "And how are you, Miss Olivia?"

"Auntie!" Olivia wrapped her arms tightly around Kira's legs.

Amanda sighed. "I guess I'm doing okay. There are still so many questions."

Kira picked Olivia up and walked into the home.

"Would you like something to eat or drink? Olivia and I had pizza for dinner. I have some wine."

"Oh, no, thank you. I'm not hungry."

"Well, let me know if you change your mind. I was thinking we can start going through Ryan's closet to look for clues."

"Oh, I didn't notice you had separate closets the last time I was here."

"Yeah, that was one of the reasons I fell in love with this house. Olivia, do you need to go potty?"

"No," murmured Olivia, who had started playing with Kira's braids.

Amanda led Kira upstairs to the bedroom. "Ryan's closet is the one on the right."

"Your closets are gorgeous. Brian may have to step up his game," Kira said as her eyes widened, staring at the closets.

"Well, I guess we can start going through the drawers and cabinets. I never come in here, so I really have no clue about what we'll find."

Kira put Olivia down. Olivia started spinning and dancing around the closet. Amanda opened one of the drawers and searched through the clothing. Kira saw a built-in computer desk in one corner of the closet. A computer, monitor, keyboard, and mouse sat on the desk. Kira wiggled the mouse to wake up the computer, but a password was required.

"Do you know the password to this computer?"

"No, but Ryan might have taped it to the desk or back of the computer. If you don't see it, let me know. I think he emailed the password to me several months ago, so I might have it saved in my cell phone."

Kira searched on and around the desk and computer. "Yeah, it looks like I will need you to check. I don't see it anywhere."

"Okay, after we look through everything else in here, I'll check."

Kira decided to focus on searching the horizontal cabinets along the wall near her head. She opened each one. Most of the cabinets contained things like towels or clothing. However, the last cabinet in the row was hidden behind a pile of clothes and, unlike the others, it was locked. "Hey, Amanda, do you have the key to this cabinet?"

"Ryan and I keep a set of keys locked in a safe. I'll go and grab Ryan's set. I'm not sure which one goes with that cabinet, so you might have to try all of them until you find the right one." Amanda left and returned with a key ring holding eight keys and handed it to Kira.

Once Kira found the correct key and unlocked the cabinet, she saw that it contained some type of security system. There were two large monitors. Kira looked closely at the monitors and noticed that one of them contained footage of her home.

"Amanda, rooms from my home are on one of these security monitors."

"What?" Amanda rushed over to Kira.

Kira pointed to the monitor. "See, that's my house. Did you know about this?"

"I haven't even been in this closet since we first moved here. I had no idea. This is strictly Ryan's closet, and I never have a reason to come in here."

Kira looked perplexed. "Why would your husband need to see inside my home?"

"I really don't know. Look, I have a feeling there's a lot I don't know about Ryan, and it doesn't help that I spend most of my time working in other countries."

"I wonder if Brian knows anything about this."

"Well, you should certainly ask him."

Amanda walked over to another drawer, opened it, and searched the contents. Her eyes began to water as she carried a few of the documents and handed them to Kira. "Here, it might be a good idea for Brian to hold onto these. It's Ryan's passport and birth certificate. Since I'm gone so much, it might be better for him to keep them in a safe place for when Ryan comes back."

Kira hugged Amanda. "Thank you. I'm sure Brian will appreciate that."

"Yeah, well, don't forget to ask him about that security system." Amanda hastily wiped a tear from her cheek and sighed. "I feel so guilty."

"What? Don't say that! You are not to blame."

"It's just that I'm never here, and I even met with a divorce attorney. Maybe if I had been here more often, our marriage would have been stronger, and this wouldn't have happened."

"Don't be ridiculous. If you had been here, you wouldn't have been able to do anything. What would you have done, fight the person who attacked him? Get real!"

Amanda's eyes blurred from the tears sticking to them. She blinked several times. "I know, but..."

The doorbell rang.

"Are you expecting someone?"

"No." Amanda picked up her cell phone to check the

doorbell camera. "I don't know who that is. Can you watch Olivia for me while I check?"

"Of course."

As Amanda walked down the stairs, she spoke through the doorbell speaker system. "May I help you?"

"Yes. My name is Detective Jones." The detective held up his badge.

"Oh, okay. I will be right with you." Amanda opened her front door. "Hello. How may I help you, Detective?"

"Can I come in?"

"Okay. What's this about?"

"I won't take up too much of your time. I'm investigating a complaint filed by Anne Walowski. Do you know her?"

"Yes, she's my daughter's nanny. Well, she was my daughter's nanny before she quit."

"I see. Well, she filed a police report against you and your husband for invasion of privacy. According to her complaint, she recently discovered security cameras in many rooms, including the bathrooms and the bedroom where she slept. I have a search warrant to search the premises." Detective Jones handed a copy of the search warrant to Amanda.

"I know we have security cameras, but I don't even know where all of them are. I travel so much for work. Ryan is the main one who would know about that."

"And Ryan is your husband who is missing?"

"That's correct. Do the police have any new information about what happened to him? It's starting to feel as if nothing is being done to find him. I had to look at a stranger's body."

"The department is following up on leads. That's all I know. I need to look around for the security cameras. Can you show me where the main security system is located?"

"Didn't you already view recordings from the cameras?"

"I'm here about cameras in the bedrooms and bathrooms."

"I don't understand what's going on." Amanda stepped aside to let the detective pass in front of her. "It's just that no one is telling me anything. I received a call to identify a body that wasn't him. Do you know how tormented I felt? I'll never live that image down. It wasn't Ryan, thank God, but where is he?"

"The department is working on your husband's case, but now I'm here to investigate Ms. Walowski's claims. Can you direct me to the bathrooms and where she slept?"

"You seem to be more concerned about her complaint than what happened to my husband. That's more serious. Did she tell you how she broke the security system?"

"Ma'am, there are other detectives working on your husband's case. And yes, she told me about what happened and why it happened. As I said, I'm just here to investigate Ms. Walowski's complaint."

"I know, but..." Amanda glanced up at the detective and noticed that he had an empathetic look on his face. She immediately relaxed and sighed. "I'm sorry. Follow me."

During the search, the detective removed some of the security cameras so that he could take it back to the station as part of his investigation. After the detective left, Amanda returned to the room with Kira and Olivia.

"What was that about?" Kira asked.

"Apparently, the nanny said something about security cameras in her bathroom and bedroom."

"You don't know anything about that?"

"No, but let me see something." Amanda left the room and returned with her laptop. "A long time ago, Ryan emailed me login information for the security system. I never used it because he took care of all that. I'm going to check my email and see if I can find it."

"Well, I think I'm going to head home. Let me know what you find out."

"Okay, I'll shoot you an email if I discover anything. I'll walk you to the door."

As she walked, Kira paused and turned toward Amanda. "You know, I don't mean to alarm you, but wouldn't it be weird if the nanny had something to do with Ryan's disappearance?"

"Oh, her? Girl, she's harmless. I wouldn't pick just anyone to trust with my daughter. I did a very thorough background check, and she came to us from a top agency."

"Okay, well, stranger things have happened. Don't forget to let me know if you find out anything," Kira said as she hugged Amanda.

"Sure, we'll talk later. Have a good evening."

Sixteen

ONE MONTH LATER

Early Saturday morning, Kira decided to do some spring cleaning by gathering unneeded household goods, old clothes, and toys for the neighborhood garage sale. She started by looking through the bedroom closet for items.

Ryan strolled into the bedroom after drinking coffee in the kitchen. As he walked, he stared at the security monitors on his cell phone.

Kira glanced at Ryan. "Hey, do you want to help me get things together for the garage sale?"

"I promised Jessica I would take her to the zoo today. She begged all evening yesterday. But I can help when we get back."

Kira smiled. She was pleasantly surprised that he wanted to leave the house. He had spent most of the month in a trance staring at four walls and the security monitors while Kira pleaded with him to seek professional help or attend the crime victims support group. "Okay, I'll try not to give away all of your things, but if you come home to empty drawers and no clothes, don't say I didn't warn you."

"I don't have a problem with that as long as you replace everything you give away. Make sure you keep a list."

"Go, get out of here!" Kira picked up a sweater and threw it at Ryan. "Hurry back so you can get to work."

"Bye!" Ryan left the bedroom and went to Jessica's room to help her get ready for the zoo.

Kira continued combing through clothes in the closet and placing unwanted items into a large, black garbage bag. She also saw some tattered shoes belonging to Brian. As she picked up a pair of them to place into the bag, she noticed that there were shoe lift insoles in them. Kira was surprised because she never thought Brian needed to be taller, but she did not think too much about it. She stuffed the shoes and the shoe lift insoles into the bag.

After Kira finished going through the closet, she walked over to the chest containing some of Brian's clothes to see if there were any clothes he no longer wore in there.

When she reached the third drawer, she saw a small, brown, leather-bound journal underneath the clothes. At first, she just left the journal alone and shut the drawer. However, after searching through the remaining two drawers, Kira returned to the third drawer and pulled out the journal. The first page of the journal read *Property of Ryan Wright.* Kira wondered why her husband would have a journal belonging to his brother, Ryan.

Kira quickly flipped through the journal and noticed that the pages were formatted like a diary with dates and details about the day's events. Kira turned to the last date in the journal. The journal's last page was dated the day *after* Ryan's disappearance. It read as follows:

May 21, 2011

I'm distraught. Brian is missing or dead, and it's probably my fault. I regret switching places with Brian. I also regret ever getting involved with stolen cars. I promise to make sure that Brian's family is taken care of, and I will do everything to make sure they have a good life. I also vow to get revenge for what happened. This morning, I took a long walk and thought about everything that happened. I'm still trying to figure everything out, and I don't know what to do. I hope and pray Brian is alive and well somewhere.

After reading the page, Kira flung the journal against the wall. There was a loud thud as the journal crashed against the wall, nicking it before it plummeted to the floor. Tears welled up in Kira's eyes. She grabbed some tissue and wiped her face as she pondered what to do. After thirty minutes passed, Kira walked to the closet, pulled out a medium-sized suitcase, and began filling it with her clothes and toiletries. Then, she rolled the suitcase to Jessica's bedroom, pulled some of Jessica's clothes out of the drawers, and stuffed them into the suitcase on top of her belongings. After packing, she loaded the suitcase into her car trunk and called a nearby hotel to book a room for the night.

Kira felt shocked and betrayed. She questioned her entire marriage. When was she with Brian, and when was she with Ryan? More importantly, was it possible that Jessica was Ryan's daughter? There were so many unanswered questions, and Kira did not have the energy to explore them. She just knew she could no longer trust either her husband or his brother.

SEVENTEEN

On his way home from the zoo, Ryan stopped by a gas station. The gas station had a mini-mart.

"Come on, honey, let's go in the store for a minute." Ryan and Jessica exited the car and walked into the mini-mart. As they entered the store, a man standing in front of the beer cooler turned and stared intensely at Ryan.

Jessica dashed over to the potato chip stand, and Ryan quickly followed behind her.

"Daddy, can I have some chips?"

"I just bought you a ton of snacks at the zoo. Aren't you stuffed?"

Jessica giggled. "This is for later when I'm not stuffed."

"Okay, you can pick a small bag." Suddenly, Ryan sensed that someone was standing close behind him. As he turned, a man bent down from the waist and smiled at Jessica.

"Well, you must be Olivia. You're just as pretty as your father said you were."

"My name is not Olivia. My name is Jessica."

"Honey, what did we teach you about talking to strangers?" Ryan glanced at the man who spoke to Jessica and immediately felt a wave of nervous energy wash over him. Ryan slowly shifted his weight as he looked at the one man who he believed may have had something to do with his brother's disappearance. Ryan immediately looked away from him as he pondered what to do.

"Ryan, you never told me you had two pretty little girls."

Ryan never noticed how dirty his shoes looked, but perhaps they became that way during his visit to the zoo. Suddenly, he felt very interested in viewing every single speck of dirt on his shoes as he muttered, "Oh, you must have me confused. I—"

"Confused? What type of game you playin'? I know you remember me with that big commission and all. Don't pretend like you don't know me, Ryan Wright. I certainly know you."

"His name is not Ryan. Daddy, tell the stranger you're not Ryan."

"I'm sorry, sir, you must have me confused with my

brother. I am definitely not Ryan, and I definitely don't know you. My name is Brian. Ryan is my twin brother."

"Twin?"

Jessica chimed in. "My daddy has an identical twin brother. They look just alike."

"Is that so? Well, Ryan didn't tell me nothin' about a twin." The man squinted his eyes and tilted his head slightly as he stared at Ryan. "You sure do look like Ryan to me, but you say you ain't him. So, it's been a while since I seen Ryan. How is he?"

"Um, I don't know. I don't know where he is," Ryan said.

"He's your twin brother, and you don't know where he is?"

"He's been missing for several weeks. No one knows where he is, but if you see him, please let him know his family is looking for him, and we miss him. Jess, come on honey. Let's go pay for these chips." After paying for the chips, Ryan clutched Jessica's hand as they walked toward the exit. The same man who had approached Ryan a few minutes ago stood in front of the door, blocking it.

"Excuse me," Ryan said as his body stiffened.

"Oh, did you hear what happened to Alex?"

"Uh, what?"

"Did you hear about Alex?"

"Alex? I don't... Oh, I don't recall my brother

mentioning an Alex." Ryan felt his fingers begin to shake. He tightened his grasp on Jessica's hand and balled his other hand into a fist to keep his fingers from moving. Suddenly, heavy raindrops poured from the cloudy sky. Ryan glanced overhead as thunder boomed through the air.

"Oh, right. You're Brian, the twin."

"Right. And what is it about Alex?"

"Oh, never mind. You don't know him anyway." The man stepped aside as Ryan and Jessica ran out of the mini-mart trying to dodge the rain. As Ryan stepped into his car, he looked over toward the mini-mart and saw the man standing outside under an awning and staring at him while he talked to someone on his cell phone and lit a cigarette. After leaving the gas station mini-mart, Ryan and Jessica returned home.

As Ryan unlocked the door, Kira grasped the journal and headed downstairs. She rushed over to Jessica.

"Hey, Jess, you got to spend all day with Daddy. Let's have some fun mommy-daughter time. Go wait for me in my car."

"Where are we going?"

"It's a surprise."

"What surprise?" Jessica's face lit up.

"Jessica, hurry and get in my car. I'll tell you all about the surprise after you get in the car." Jessica finally opened the door and skipped to Kira's car.

Ryan looked perplexed. "What's going on?"

Kira threw the journal at Ryan, striking him in the chest, and stomped out the door, slamming it shut behind her. After checking into the hotel, Kira sat on the bed and perused the room service menu.

"When are we going home, Mommy?"

"I don't know. Let's have a fun vacation. Are you hungry?"

"No. Is Daddy coming too?"

"No, this is a girls' trip. Only girls are going on this vacation. Did you eat something at the zoo?"

"Yeah." Jessica bounced onto the bed and sat down next to Kira.

"What did you eat? Would you like some dessert? They have chocolate cake," Kira said as she flipped through the room service menu.

"I ate a hot dog and French fries. Can I have some cake?"

"Sure, I will order some cake for you and a sandwich for me." Kira's cell phone began ringing nonstop. Finally, the ringing stopped, only to be replaced with constant text message alerts. Kira picked up the phone and turned it off. "Would you like to go to the movies?"

"Yes. Is Daddy going to come to the movies too?"

"No, remember, this is for girls only. After I eat, we'll go to the movies. Maybe I'll find some cartoons for you to watch now." Kira picked up the TV remote control and flipped through the channels until she found a kid-friendly cartoon. Then she phoned room service and ordered a chicken club sandwich, fruit salad, and a piece of cake for Jessica.

After eating, Kira took Jessica to a nearby shopping mall, where they did a little shopping and went to see a movie. After returning to the hotel from the mall, Jessica went to sleep, and Kira finally turned on her cell phone. There were fifteen missed calls from Ryan and ten text messages. As Kira clicked to view a text message, her phone rang. The caller ID said "Brian."

Kira pressed the button to answer the call. "I have nothing to say to you."

"I just want to apologize."

"Did you even bother to think about the consequences of your actions?"

"I just want to explain. Brian and I had a unique relationship."

"There are no excuses for the lies."

"I guess we just thought of ourselves as one person. We never intended to hurt anyone."

"So, what were your plans? Were you planning to take over Brian's life forever?"

"I planned to switch back when he returned. I never wanted to hurt you or Jessica or Olivia or Amanda. We switched places for so long. I guess we grew to believe we were the same person."

"There are no excuses. It's one thing to play games as a kid, but you're too old for that. It's not just about you. You have a wife and child, whoever you are. And by the way, do you even know which one of you is Jessica and Olivia's father?"

Ryan felt his blood boil, "Does it matter? Does any of this even matter right now?"

"I can't believe you even asked that! Of course, it matters. It matters to the children, and it should matter to you too. I'm sure Amanda would also like to know who she was sleeping with."

"My brother is missing. That's all that really matters right now. You act like you're not even concerned about your husband. Look, we're identical. Do you know what that means? Genetically, we are the same, but that doesn't even matter right now. The only thing that matters is that the most important person in my life is gone."

"You are one twisted, sick..."

"Can you at least try to understand my point of view?"

"There's nothing to understand," Kira huffed.

"Regardless of what you may think or feel right now, Brian and I have been great husbands and fathers," Ryan said hoarsely.

"You lied! You and Brian have been scammers! Scam artists, that's what you are." Kira quickly hung up her phone.

"Mommy, what's a scam artist?"

Jessica's sweet-sounding voice startled Kira. She turned around and saw Jessica standing there with her eyes half closed. Kira was not sure what her daughter heard or even what she understood. "Oh, nothing, baby. You don't need to worry about that now."

"Am I a scam artist?"

Kira pulled Jessica closer and hugged her gently. "Oh, no. You're a sweet angel. Now, let's get back to bed. Did I wake you up?"

"Yeah," Jessica said as she yawned and rubbed her eyes.

"Oh, I'm sorry about that. I'll be quiet so you can sleep." Kira walked with Jessica back to the bed and tucked her in. Kira also got in the bed, turned off the lamp, and went to sleep.

In the morning, Kira ordered breakfast. While Jessica was eating, Kira carried her cell phone into the bathroom and called her friend Karen.

"Hey, girl, what's up?"

"Hi, Karen. Ryan and I had a big fight last night."

"Wait, what? You had a fight with your brother-in-law? He came back?"

"Oh, did I say Ryan? I meant Brian. Brian and I had a big argument last night. Jessica and I spent the night in a hotel."

"What happened?"

"I found out that Brian and Ryan have been switching places."

"Isn't that what identical twins do? You know they're jokesters." Karen could be heard smacking and popping gum while talking.

"Um, I never really thought of them as jokesters. Besides, they lied to everyone," Kira said.

"A lot of twins trick people by switching places. Okay, girl, spill the dirt. Did he cheat on you? Is that what this is really about?"

"It's not about cheating. I don't even know if there was any cheating. It's about dishonesty. I can't trust someone who lies to me. And there's an even bigger question. Where is my husband? Brian's the one who's actually missing. To be honest, I'm so pissed about what he and his brother did, I don't know if I even care about where he is right now. But I worry about Jessica. I'm not trying to be selfish. Olivia deserves a father too, but—"

"Wait, I'm confused. I thought Ryan was the missing one."

Kira lowered her voice. "Okay, don't tell anyone, but I found out that Brian is the one who's actually missing because they had switched places. Ryan has been pretending to be Brian."

"Wow. I don't even know what to say. That's like some crazy soap opera shit. Well, let me know if you need a good divorce lawyer. I know someone who's superb. And if you need a place to crash, I'm here for you."

"I don't think I'm ready to go there yet."

"Yeah, well, let me know. I will pray for you. I'm sure everything will work itself out. Girl, I'm gonna get off this phone. Mimosas are calling my name. Feel free to call me anytime you need to talk. I'm here for you. Hey, why don't you join me? We can discuss everything during brunch."

"Thanks, but I'm going to distract Jessica by planning a fun day with her. We'll talk later. Remember, do not tell anyone."

"My lips are sealed."

"I know how you can be sometimes. Do not tell anyone." Kira wished she hadn't told Karen everything about the twins. After all, Karen had been known to reveal secrets in the past. What was she thinking? "Karen, it's really important for no one else to know right now."

"Girl, bye."

The next morning, Kira checked out of the hotel and dropped Jessica off at school. Then she drove home, dropped off her luggage, and went to work. After work, Kira picked Jessica up from the after-school program, picked up a pizza for dinner, and went home. Ryan still had not returned home. While Jessica was busy eating dinner, Kira dragged a huge suitcase out of her bedroom closet and stuffed it with Ryan's clothes and personal care products. She dragged the suitcase down the stairs and placed it next to the kitchen door.

One hour later, Ryan arrived home. As soon as he walked in the door, he glanced down at the suitcase.

"I'm so glad you're back." Ryan stretched out his arms to hug Kira.

Kira immediately turned her back to Ryan. "I packed your clothes in that suitcase. Take it and leave."

"Where am I supposed to go?"

Kira could feel her blood boil. She took a deep breath. "That is not my problem. You have a wife and a child. I'm sure they will be happy to see you. Frankly, I really don't care where you go."

"I'll give you time to cool off. You know I can't go back to my old life."

"Just tell Amanda the truth."

"Whoever attacked or killed my brother will come after me if they find out the truth."

Kira threw her hands up in the air. "Not my problem."

"Surely you don't feel that way."

"Bye!" Kira quickly flicked her hand at Ryan.

Ryan raised the suitcase handle, opened the door, and slowly rolled the suitcase out of the house. He decided to stay in a hotel until he could figure out how to convince Kira to take him back.

After Ryan left, Kira helped Jessica with her homework.

"Mommy."

"Yes, Jessica?"

"When will Daddy be home?"

"I don't know, honey. Let's finish your work so you can have some playtime before bed." After Jessica finished her homework, they played with Jessica's dollhouse before going to sleep. In the morning, Kira helped Jessica get ready for school.

Kira started combing Jessica's hair. "Jessica, are you excited about your upcoming birthday party?"

"Yeah."

"Hopefully, your friends will be able to come. I ordered your cake yesterday. So, what do you want for your birthday?"

"Um, I want a doll."

"Anything else?"

"I don't know."

"That's okay. I'm sure I'll be able to find something nice for you."

After Kira finished Jessica's hair, Jessica stood up and began skipping around the house looking in every room.

"Jessica, what are you doing? Stop running around."

"Where's Daddy?"

"Oh, he's not here. Come, let's eat breakfast."

"I want to tell him something before he goes exercise."

"Well, let's go eat. What did you want to tell Daddy?"

"Ah, what I want for my birthday. Mommy, you know. I have to tell Daddy. I have to tell Daddy what I want for my birthday."

"Okay, well, you have to get ready to go to school. Maybe I'll let you call him after you eat, but you have to eat all of your cereal." After Jessica finished eating her cereal, Kira dialed Ryan's phone number on her cell phone and held the phone out to Jessica when he answered.

Jessica yanked the phone out of Kira's hand. "Daddy?"

"Hi, baby. How are you?"

"Daddy, where are you?"

"I'm at a hotel."

"Are you on vacation?"

"Yes, I'm on—"

"Look, Daddy, I want to tell you what I want for my birthday."

Kira glanced at her watch. "Jessica, hurry up. It's almost time for the bus to come."

"Okay, Daddy, I have to go, but I want to tell you what I want for my birthday. You remember the doll we saw with the blue dress? I want that one."

"Okay, honey. I'll let you go so you can get on the bus. I love you."

"I love you too. Bye!"

"Bye, baby."

Jessica handed the phone to Kira and dashed away to get her book bag and jacket before heading to the school bus.

Two weeks later, Kira helped Jessica get dressed in a pretty, pink dress for her birthday party. Amanda came to the party early with Olivia to help Kira set out tables and chairs and decorations in the backyard. Margaret, the twins' mother, was the next party guest to arrive. Other guests gradually trickled in until there were twenty party-goers, including children and adults. After the party started, Ryan arrived lugging a large box wrapped in paper covered with pictures of balloons. As he entered the back-yard, Jessica ran up to him and tightly wrapped her arms around him.

"Hey, Jessie! I missed you so much!"

"I missed you too, Daddy. When are you coming home?"

"Hopefully soon. I hope to come home soon. Where's your mommy?"

"Ah, I don't know. I think she might be in the house."

Ryan turned to the right and noticed a table with several gifts and a card box on it. "Okay, I'm going to put your gift down and look for Mommy." As Ryan walked to the gift table, Amanda walked up behind him.

"Hello, brother-in-law."

Ryan turned around and looked at Amanda. He quickly placed the gift on the table and gave her a hug. "Hey, Amanda. How is everything?"

"I have my good days and my bad days, but overall things are okay given the circumstances. I'm planning to take Olivia on some of my work trips. I just need to locate a nanny or daycare provider to take care of her while I work. How have you been?"

"They say it gets easier, but I never even imagined a life without my brother. I just hope to get some answers about what happened to him soon. Hopefully, some good news."

"I must admit, it's a little unnerving looking at my husband's twin while my husband is nowhere to be found, and I'm starting to worry about Olivia. She's too young to understand anything, and she sometimes asks about her daddy." Amanda glanced over at Olivia as she ran around the yard. Then she looked at Jessica laughing and dancing with a small group of friends. "Well, we're here to celebrate

Jessica. I don't want to take away from that," Amanda said.

"It was great seeing you again, Amanda. If you ever need anything, let me know. I know I can't take his place, but I never want Olivia to be without a father figure in her life. I will always be there for her." Ryan felt a pang of guilt hearing Amanda talk about her missing husband. He wondered what would happen if he told her the truth. He knew Amanda was an independent woman who seemed to put work above everything else, but he never doubted her love of him and Olivia. Would she ever forgive him?

"Thank you. I'm sure we won't need anything, but thanks for the offer." Olivia jogged up to Amanda. "Hey, babe, are you having fun?"

"Yes!"

"Say hi to Uncle Brian."

"Daddy?"

"No, this is your uncle Brian. Your daddy isn't here, honey." Amanda reached down and picked Olivia up. "Do you remember your uncle Brian?"

Olivia frowned. "He looks like Daddy."

Ryan bent down in front of Olivia and grabbed her hands; he swung her arms gently. "Hello, Olivia. How are you? Are you having fun at Jessica's birthday party?"

"Yeah." Olivia nervously looked down at her hands as Ryan touched them.

"That's great. Are you ready to eat some cake?"

"Yeah," Olivia mumbled.

"Ollie, what's wrong?" Amanda glanced at Ryan and smiled. "I don't know why she's suddenly acting shy." Amanda set Olivia down on the grass, and Olivia dashed away toward a group of children.

Ryan chuckled. "Yeah, you never know with kids. Do you know where Kira is?"

"I think she's in the house getting ready to bring the birthday cake out."

"Okay, thanks." Ryan turned and walked into the home. Kira was in the kitchen sticking candles into the birthday cake.

"Do you need help with anything?"

Without looking up, Kira continued inserting the candles. "No, I'm good."

"We need to work this through. Don't you at least miss me a little?"

"No. Well, maybe just a little. A tiny, tiny bit just because I'm used to you being here. I'm doing perfectly okay without you," Kira scoffed.

"That may be true, but I'm sure you would be doing more than perfectly okay with me here."

"Say what you want. That doesn't make it true."

"You know Jessica would be happier with a father in her life. She would be happier with me in her life. You also know I cannot go back to my past life. It's not even an option."

"I can't talk about this now." Kira picked up the cake and walked toward the door. Ryan opened the door and held it open for Kira to walk through.

After all the guests had left the party, Ryan approached Kira. "I know you're still upset with me. Please know that Brian and I meant no ill will. We wanted the best for you and Amanda and the children. I don't know how to explain things."

"So, you're going to stand there and try to justify your lies?"

"I don't really see it as a lie. It's just that sometimes I am Ryan and sometimes I am Brian. That's who I am. That's not a lie. It's the same with Brian. We really see ourselves as one person. I guess it's like we're one person with two bodies."

"Well, I'm only married to one person, and that person is Brian, not you!"

"I am Brian now. That's who I am. When I go to work, I am Brian. At home, I am Brian. When I go to the mini-mart and see someone who wants me dead as Ryan, I am Brian. Being Ryan again is not an option."

"Okay, I don't know what you did at the mini-mart, but you and your brother are two people—two separate people. You have two separate bodies, two separate brains, two separate souls. It's like you're delusional or something. I don't even know what to think; I'm too tired. I've had a long day, and I'm too tired to even think about this right now."

Jessica ran up to Ryan carrying a large box that filled her arms. "Daddy, will you play this game with me?"

"I don't know, honey. I don't think Mommy wants me to stay tonight," Ryan said as he glanced at Kira.

"Please stay. Mommy, please can Daddy stay tonight? I promise to be good."

"Jessi—"

"Please, Mommy. Pretty please." Jessica skipped in front of Kira and pressed her hands together and folded her fingers in prayer format as she pleaded.

Kira sighed. "I guess he can stay tonight since it's your birthday." Kira walked up to Ryan and whispered into his ear, "Sleep in the guest room."

Ryan nodded. "Thank you. Come on, Jessica. I'll play the game with you."

"It's almost her bedtime. Don't keep her up late."

Ryan spent a couple of hours playing with Jessica before retreating to bed in the guest room.

Eighteen

The doctor discharged Brian. He still had no memory about his past life. Occasionally, he remembered the image of a person or location, but he had no idea who or what they were. He also did not remember his actual name, so he decided to come up with a name that was simple and easy to remember. He thought about the names of doctors and nurses he heard in the hospital, but he was having difficult time remembering most of them.

Nurse Paulina saw Brian standing near the hospital's exit. "Hey, sir. I bet you're excited. You get to leave this dump."

"I don't know about that."

"Do you have somewhere to stay?"

"No. I guess that's why I'm nervous about leaving. I don't know where to go. Nothing seems familiar."

"Well, you're in luck. I have a cousin who owns a boardinghouse. It's not too far."

"Thank you, but I have no money."

"Don't worry about it. We'll work something out. I have a large family. I can ask around. I'm sure someone has a job somewhere."

"That would really be great. I don't know what I can do yet, but I will be a hard worker."

"Do you mind hanging around for an hour? I can drive you to my cousin's place when I get off work. Maybe you can hang out in the cafeteria until my shift ends."

"Yes, thank you again."

Paulina reached into her pocket, pulled out twenty pesos, and handed the money to Brian. "Here. I don't have much cash with me, but maybe you can buy a snack or some coffee."

"Thank you!" Brian crumpled the money in his hand and walked to the cafeteria to wait for Paulina's shift to end. In the cafeteria, Brian purchased a cup of coffee and churros. After a little more than one hour passed, Paulina came to the cafeteria.

"I'm done with work. Are you ready to get out of this place?"

"Sure." Brian stood up and followed Paulina out of the hospital.

"Well, my cousin is Rosa. She and her husband, Javier, have three extra rooms in their home that they rent out. You're in luck because one of their tenants just moved out two weeks ago. They are very nice. The room is very nice. You will like it there."

"I'm just happy to have someplace to go."

Paulina led Brian to her car. She unlocked the doors, and they entered it.

"Rosa said you can stay there as long as you want. You don't need to pay anything until you find a job."

"No problem. As soon as I find a job, I will pay."

"My uncle works at a resort. I'll ask him if he knows about any jobs. Do you have any memory about what you used to do? Or do you remember going to a school or college?"

"I really don't remember. I believe I went to school, but I don't remember anything." Brian smiled as he gazed at Paulina's face. She seemed like an angel. Not only was she beautiful, but she was doing everything to help him. His gaze was cut short when Paulina caught him staring at her.

"That's okay. I'm sure someone will find work for you. I'm sure Rosa and Javier will appreciate it if you help them around the house for now."

"Sure, I will help with everything."

"Since you don't remember your actual name, what should I call you?"

"I don't know. What do you like?"

"Well, in the hospital we referred to you as a John Doe. What if we call you Juan? That's another name for John. Do you like that name?"

Brian shrugged. "It sounds good to me."

"Okay, Juan. We're almost there." Five minutes later, Paulina drove up to Rosa's house. As Brian and Paulina got out of the car, Rosa jogged toward them waving her hand. As soon as she reached Paulina, she hugged her tightly.

"Hi, Rosa, this is my friend Juan."

"Welcome, Juan. I bet you're happy to get out of that old hospital."

"Yes, ma'am."

"Oh, call me Rosa. Ma'am is for old ladies. Besides, we're family now. I hope both of you are good and hungry. Come in and get some food."

Brian smiled. He could not remember what it was like to have a home, but Rosa's warmth made him feel at home.

"I hope you didn't go through too much trouble," Paulina said as she followed Rosa into the home.

"Nonsense! Now, there is plenty of food. Paulina, you make sure you fix a plate to take home," Rosa exclaimed.

Javier approached Paulina and said, "There is so much food we can feed ten football teams." Javier chuckled.

"Juan, this is my husband, Javier. Javier, Juan is going to stay in the extra room."

Javier turned toward Juan. "Welcome, Juan. Is your luggage in the car?"

"Oh, um, I don't really have anything." Brian held up the plastic hospital bag filled with the dirty clothes he had on when he first went to the hospital along with his hospital discharge instructions and his medication. "This is all I have."

"He just got out of the hospital," Paulina piped up, "but I'm working on getting some things for him. A few of my co-workers are dropping off some of their old clothes tomorrow."

"Well, Juan, let me show you your room. Follow me."

As Brian followed behind Javier, he looked around the home and thought about how colorful everything seemed. It was certainly different than the stark whiteness of the hospital. Brian didn't remember ever seeing such a colorful home, but he was not sure if that was because he had lost his memory. Most of the walls were a burnt orange color, and they were covered with many photographs and paintings. It was clear Rosa and Javier loved art and decorations. The home was a ranch-style home with all rooms on one level. Brian expected to go upstairs to the bedroom, so he was surprised when Javier led him to a room without going up any stairs. Brian seemed to remember going upstairs to go to sleep, but he could not remember anything about what his past bedroom looked like or where it was located. He just remembered walking up a lot of stairs.

Javier led Brian through a long hallway, past two bedrooms, to a small bedroom with blue walls, a full-size bed, a small chest of drawers, and a small walk-in closet. "I hope everything meets with your liking. We don't mind if you paint the walls a different color. There's a linen closet next to the bathroom if you need towels. You will share the bathroom with the other boarders, but don't worry. They work a lot, so you should be able to use the bathroom whenever you want."

After showing Brian his bedroom, Javier led Brian to the kitchen where there was a long counter covered with pots and aluminum pans of varying sizes. Javier grabbed a plate from an overhead cabinet. Then he reached into a drawer, pulled out a fork and spoon, and handed them to Brian. "We have a ton of food. Enchiladas, tamales, chicken, rice, and fajitas. Get as much as you want."

After piling his plate with food, Brian sat at the dining

room table next to Paulina. Rosa sat at the table across from him. "So, Juan, are you single?"

Paulina looked up from her plate. "Rosa! That's not your business."

"What? He's going to be living here. There's nothing wrong with getting to know him, so he won't be a stranger. Besides, I may know a single lady or two. And you're single. Don't you want to know?"

"He will tell me what he wants me to know. And I told you about his memory."

"Okay then, Juan, do you remember if you're single?"

"Rosa!" Paulina rolled her eyes.

Brian chuckled. "No, it's okay. No, I really don't know if I'm single. I would hope I would remember having a wife or girlfriend if I really had one, but I really don't know."

"Well, if you don't remember, that's a sign. Let me see your hand." Rosa leaned forward, reaching toward Brian.

"Excuse me?" Brian said.

"Come on, let me see your hands. I want to see if there's a tan line for a wedding ring." Rosa wiggled her hand. Brian stretched both of his hands out toward Rosa. She grabbed his hands and slowly inspected each finger. "I don't know. I think there might be signs of a tan line on this one finger, but no, maybe not. I can't really tell."

Paulina sipped some of her water. "I can't believe you. Just leave this poor man alone!"

"If you don't remember, that's a sign the wife or girl-friend was not good for you. There were bad things. A poor life. Your mind wanted to rid you of that life so you could move on and find happiness. Perhaps find happiness with a new woman. I know some nice single ladies. And Paulina, she's single. She might not be good for you, though, because she wants to stay single," Rosa exclaimed.

"That's not true!" Paulina stood and carried her plate into the kitchen. "I have an early shift, so I'm going to wrap up this food and leave."

"Yeah, it's true. I introduced her to ten men and nothing. She's still single. Ten men. Ten single men. They were good men too."

"Bye, Rosa. I'm not even going to go into that with you. Bye, Javier. Juan, I will check on you tomorrow. You can let me know if Rosa is driving you crazy. If so, I can find someplace else for you to live."

Brian squinted and wracked his brain as he tried to remember if he had been married. He had no memory of being married, but he felt as if he had attended at least one wedding. He could not remember if he had been a groom or a guest.

The next evening, Paulina dropped off donated clothes and toiletries for Brian. After carrying the items to his bedroom, Brian sat down in the living room on the sofa. Paulina walked into the living room and sat down next to Brian.

"Juan, have you heard anything from the police about finding your family?"

"I only talked to them at the hospital. They only seemed to be interested in arresting me."

"For what?"

"I have no idea. They accused me of lying about not remembering anything. They said they were investigating me for criminal activity."

"Well, you don't seem like any type of criminal to me," Paulina said. "I mean, you don't have any physical signs of someone who's been in a lot of fights, and there are no signs of drug or alcohol abuse. Your test results seem to suggest a healthy lifestyle, and despite being found in a dump site, your nails look manicured."

"That's good to know," Brian said as he smiled curtly.

"Hey, I have a neighbor who works as a reporter for a local newspaper. Are you willing to be interviewed by him? There has to be someone out there who recognizes you. Perhaps by putting out a news report with your picture, we can locate your family and find out who you are."

Brian smiled. "Sure, that sounds like a great idea."

One week later, Brian met with the reporter, and an article about him was published on the front page of *El Sol de Tijuana* the following day. He spent the next several days fielding phone calls from other local reporters and answering questions during television interviews. At the end of the week, Paulina decided to give Brian a tour of the city and treat him to a picnic lunch in the park. After lunch in the park, they walked to the adjoining beach. As they walked toward the water's edge, Paulina paused for a moment and bent down to slip off her shoes. When she stood again, she found Brian looking at her lovingly. *She is so beautiful*, he thought.

Paulina briefly looked into Brian's eyes and grinned. For the first time, she realized how handsome he looked. The scars and bruises on his face did not take away from his appeal. "What's on your mind?"

Realizing that Paulina noticed him looking at her, Brian fidgeted and wrung his shaky hands out in front of his body. "Oh, I'm sorry. I didn't mean to stare."

"Don't worry. You didn't do anything wrong." A gust of wind punched Paulina in the face, almost knocking her over. "Ooh, this wind is starting to really pick up. It's starting to get a little chilly out here."

Brian gently wrapped his arms around Paulina. "Does this help?"

Paulina pulled Brian closer into a tight hug and leaned her head against his chest. "Definitely."

"So, is it true what Rosa said?"

"Oh, you can't go by anything she says. She just runs that big mouth of hers. Wait, what are you talking about?"

"When she said you want to stay single."

Paulina felt her cheeks warm as they flushed. "Like I said, you can't pay attention to her. She doesn't know what she's talking about."

After several minutes, Brian reached out and lifted Paulina's chin. Looking deep into her eyes, he leaned in and kissed her on the lips. He pulled away. "I'm sorry. I didn't mean to—"

Paulina put her index finger up to Brian's lips. "Shh." She reached up, pulled his face closer, and returned his kiss.

They continued to walk along the water with Brian's right arm wrapped around Paulina's shoulder. Suddenly, a figure dressed in black appeared in Brian's peripheral vision. Brian shuffled sideways to let him pass. *Strange*, he thought, *that man almost walked right into me.*

In a dark blur, he felt the man rush him, delivering a right hook to his jaw. Crack. "Juan!" Paulina screamed, reaching for her cell phone. The man snatched it from her hands, threw it into the water, and brandished a pistol. "Step back," he warned in a gruff voice. His face was nondescript, shaded by his hood.

"Please don't hurt her," Brian said hoarsely, his head spinning while his jaw throbbed. The man grabbed him by his shirt collar and began zip-tying his hands together. The man shoved Brian into the sand, zip-tied his ankles together, and slapped a piece of duct tape over his mouth. He hoisted him onto his shoulder and carried him up the beach into the parking lot, where an undistinguished black van sat overlooking the ocean. He opened the trunk and shoved Brian into the back. The van rumbled as it started, and Brian's head collided with something blunt as the man sped off.

Brian panicked and terror set in. *What in the world is going on?* he thought. He struggled against his binds, feeling faint as he passed out into blackness.

When Brian awoke, a blinding pain crashed into his temples, so powerful he thought he might lose consciousness again. For a second, he couldn't remember where he was, or anything from the last twenty-four hours. His cheek was pressed against a cold floor, and all he could see in front of him was a dark, industrial room. Brian wiggled and felt the bite of zip ties against his wrists and ankles. The claustrophobia of being bound made his chest tighten, and a creeping feeling of dread sat in his stomach. He wanted to scream, but his throat felt like barbed wire.

Brian perked up as he heard a clamoring of footsteps and indistinct voices from above. A door creaked. Brian flinched as heavy shoes smacked against the stairs.

Three figures came into view, difficult to make out in

the darkness of the room. Two were of average height and brawny, while the one in the middle was tall and lithe. Chairs squeaked obnoxiously on the concrete floor as they sat down. Someone fumbled with a switch, and the room flooded with light, pricking at Brian's eyes.

The three men stared at Brian with a twisted fascination. "Looks like Sleeping Beauty's awake," the one on the right jeered, lighting a cigarette. The man in the middle rolled his eyes and moved from his seat to kneel in front of Brian's face. He had olive skin, thin, smirking lips, and a scatter of stubble framing his face. The most striking were his eyes: deep chocolate brown, with an unexpected vulnerability behind them. He looked to be in his early thirties.

"I know you remember me," he cocked an eyebrow as he ripped the duct tape off Brian's mouth.

"No," Brian mumbled.

The man's brow furrowed, and he grabbed Brian roughly by the neck, sitting him upright. "Look me in the eyes when I speak to you," he seethed. "I'm going to ask you some questions, and if you don't tell me the truth, you'll regret it."

"Okay." Brian raised his gaze tentatively.

"You sold a candy red Maserati to Veronica Kameron almost a year ago. Who sold it to you?"

Brian still felt faint and struggled to regain an ounce of alertness. "I-I don't know. You may have me mistaken."

"You don't know? You don't know? You don't remember my beautiful wife's car? Where did you buy that car, or did you steal it, you piece of scum?"

Before Brian could register anything or respond, the man swung at his mouth with intense force. The pain was excruciating. Blood splattered from his mouth, and a rogue tooth fell out onto the floor.

"That car you sold me was stolen from an extremely dangerous man with a lot of enemies. Whoever sold it to you is scum, and trust me, whatever allegiance you have to him won't matter if you keep lying to me," he warned, searching Brian's face.

"Don't know," Brian gasped, feeling dizzy. "I have no memory." Suddenly, Brian had a vision of himself standing in a car showroom looking at shiny, new cars. There were five cars arranged in a semicircle; many were sports cars.

The three men laughed in unison. The more Brian studied the inquisitor's gait and voice, the more he seemed like the one who had kidnapped him. Brian passed out. One of the men grabbed Brian's shoulders and shook him, but he remained unconscious.

NINETEEN

Paulina stood dumbfounded. She shook herself to try and snap out of it and sprinted after the car, but by the time she reached the parking lot, they were gone. The warm breeze caught a piece of paper, and Paulina grabbed it as it flew past her face. As she glanced at the paper, she quickly realized it was the news report her neighbor had released about Juan. She immediately made her way to his office.

Paulina stormed into her neighbor's office in a flash, smacking the paper on his desk.

"Jorge, what happened?" she asked accusingly. "He's gone!"

"Whoa, slow down, who's gone?"

"Juan!" Paulina burst into tears. "We were walking

along the beach when someone attacked him, tied him up, and threw him into the back of a car!"

Jorge was stunned. "Paulina, I can assure you, I don't know anything about what happened. I will see if I can get to the bottom of it." He picked up the phone and dialed furiously.

Paulina, frustrated and visibly upset, snatched the phone out of his hands, cleared the receiver, and dialed her cousin Rosa. After Paulina explained what happened, Rosa offered to call friends and family to see if anyone knew anything. "I'll have everyone meet at my house. Don't worry, we'll find him, my love."

Paulina and Jorge drove to Rosa's house. Before long, the house was filled with people. Every few minutes, someone entered the home.

"*Hermana*? I'm here!" Paulina's sister, Carla, called as she let herself into the house, dragging an oversized bag that looked like the kind of thing you'd pack for a month's vacation. Paulina rushed to greet her sister and gave her a big hug.

"I am so glad you're here!" Paulina cried as a sense of relief seemed to overcome her. Paulina's eyes began to well up with tears.

"We'll find him, don't worry," Carla said as she embraced her sister.

Paulina's cousin Martina entered the room and said,

"Hey, guys, I think I have something." Everyone stopped talking and turned their gaze toward Martina. "So, you know Miguel, my co-worker I told you about? Well, anyway, his sister saw something suspicious when she was walking her dog. She saw someone carrying someone who looked like Juan into a house. At first, she couldn't tell it was a person or some type of animal."

"Where was this house?" Rosa piped up.

"I believe it was a few blocks from where she lived. Maybe we can meet Miguel's sister and have her show us the house," Martina said.

"Okay, everyone, let's go!" Paulina jumped up and headed toward the front door.

Jorge stepped in front of the door, blocking her. "Wait, everyone, we don't know what we're going into. They might have weapons, and we don't know how many people are there."

"Okay, then, we'll get weapons. Everyone grab a weapon and meet at Miguel's sister's house in thirty minutes. Get whatever you have—guns, knives, broomsticks, Mace, or golf clubs. Martina, tell everyone where to go," Rosa said.

Thirty minutes later, everyone gathered in the front yard of Miguel's sister's house. Two people followed Miguel and his sister to the home to survey what was there. There were no people outside, and there was one vehicle parked in front that fit the description of the one Paulina saw driving away with Brian. When they returned from the survey, everyone piled into their cars and followed Miguel.

After arriving at the home, half of the people snuck around the back, and the other half converged in the front yard. Some of the people tiptoed up to the windows and peeked in to see if they could see anyone. One person saw two men sitting at a kitchen table eating.

Suddenly, someone from inside opened the front door and stepped out. When he saw the people in his front yard, he pulled a gun out of his pocket and started shooting at them. Everyone scattered, and those with guns started firing back. The men who were in the kitchen ran outside and fired shots. Paulina snuck up behind one of the men and struck him in the head with a shovel. Then she and Miguel darted into the home while everyone else was distracted.

Paulina and Miguel frantically searched several rooms before finding one with a locked door. Paulina used her shovel to break the door lock. When she opened the door, she saw Brian lying on the floor motionless.

"Juan!" Paulina cried, as she rushed to embrace him. "Help me untie him!"

Brian took a deep breath as he looked at Paulina in amazement. "How did you find me?"

"Someone saw you being carried into the house. Hurry, let's get out of here."

Miguel yanked his knife out of his pant pocket and used it to untie Brian. Next, Miguel and Paulina led Brian out of the home with each of his arms over one of their shoulders. When they made it outside, some of the other people gathered around Brian and helped carry him to Paulina's car.

Suddenly, one of the kidnappers ran from the back of the house and started shooting in Paulina's direction. Paulina and Miguel quickly shoved Brian into the car and jumped in after him. Paulina sped away as the gunman shot toward her car, striking the bumper. The gunman ran and continued shooting at Paulina's car until he ran out of bullets. Some of Paulina's family members caught up to him and tackled him to the ground. Several police cars arrived with loud sirens wailing and parked in front of the house.

After driving a few miles and checking the rearview mirror to make sure she wasn't being followed, Paulina turned toward Miguel. "Miguel, do you want me to drop you off at home?"

"Sure, that would be great."

After dropping Miguel off at home, Paulina drove throughout the night for hours without a plan for where she was heading, while Brian slept. As the sun peeked over the horizon, Brian peeled open his eyes.

Brian looked at Paulina. "Where are we going?"

Paulina smiled. "Well, hello there. We are going to get you as far away from your kidnappers as possible."

"Where's that?" Brian sounded groggy.

"I don't know, but we'll stop at the next hotel we see to get some rest."

"Okay. Sounds good." Brian gave Paulina the thumbs-up.

After driving for one more hour, Paulina found a small hotel and checked into a room. She helped Brian walk into the room by letting him lean on her. "We'll stay here for a couple of days." Paulina grabbed a washcloth and put a pile of ice in it from the ice machine. She handed it to Brian to put against his head. Then Paulina called Rosa for updates.

"Hey, Rosa. This is Paulina. I'm calling from a hotel phone. What happened after we left?"

"Well, there are two dead men. I don't know who they are. One man escaped. During the fight, someone threw something on fire toward the house and it exploded. We made it away okay. A couple of people were shot, but they'll be okay. Everyone made it out alive. Why are you at a hotel?"

"To get away from whomever is after Juan. Now, I'm

especially worried since you said one of the men was able to get away. We don't know where he is, so we're staying away until it's safe." Paulina walked over to the window and peeked out between the curtains.

Rosa yawned. "Yeah, right." Rosa yawned again. "Well, it's time for me to go to bed now. I'm about to fall asleep any second."

The following morning, Paulina called Jorge and told him she ran away with Juan to find someplace safe to live. Jorge agreed to publish a news article stating that the unidentified man he previously wrote about had been killed in the fire. Paulina's family and friends collected money and wired it to her.

Paulina and Brian ordered room service.

"Juan, do you have any idea why those men were after you? Did you know them?"

"They mentioned something about a car I sold. I don't remember selling a car. I didn't know who they were, but they seemed to know me."

"It's odd that someone would kidnap someone over a car. Do you think you were a car salesman?"

Brian's shoulders flinched a tight shrug. "I have no idea."

Paulina giggled. "Ah, I hope you weren't a used car salesman."

"Why is that?"

"You know what they say about used car salesmen. Or maybe you don't remember. Anyway, nobody likes a used car salesman."

Brian laughed. "I'm not a used car salesman now, so you can like me. Note to self—find a non-used car sales job."

"Well, when you get all healed up, I can help you find a job. I have a large family. If you want a job as a car salesman, I'm sure one of my relatives can help with that."

Brian chuckled. "I think it may be best for me to stay away from selling cars given what happened. What about you? Don't you have to go back to your job at the hospital?"

"Well, I do love my job, but I love my life even more. Whoever went after you saw me." Paulina noticed Brian's worried expression. "Don't worry. I can find a job at a different hospital. They always need nurses."

"Well, thank you so much for everything. Thank you for saving me. Thank you for giving me a new life. I really appreciate it."

"That's what friends are for, and I'm a nurse. I'm used to taking care of people, even people who don't know who they are." Paulina grinned and winked at Brian.

That next day, Brian decided to surprise Paulina. He spent the entire morning walking around the block picking wildflowers to give to her. The hotel concierge had told him about a nearby beach and arranged for a private shuttle to take Brian and Paulina there. Brian handed Paulina the flowers and told her he had a surprise for her as he led her to the hotel shuttle. Paulina desperately wanted to know where he was taking her, but he was determined to keep it a surprise. After some time, the shuttle parked near the beach.

"Do you see that boat?" Brian asked.

"The grande one way out there? Si," Paulina replied. "What about it?"

"Well, the concierge was kind enough to arrange a short boat cruise. He'd heard about what happened to us and even had the restaurant make us some sandwiches to enjoy during the cruise."

Paulina's eyes lit up. "Oh, Juanito! That's amazing! I can't wait!" she exclaimed. Suddenly, her excitement turned to worry. "Wait, how did he hear? How much does he know?"

"I may have told him a little something without providing too many details." Brian looked at her and winked. "Look, we don't have anything to worry about. The concierge seemed like a really nice guy. He even said something about making sure we had our privacy." Brian and Paulina hopped out of the shuttle, grabbed the bag with the sandwiches, and made their way down to where the boat was docked. The views from the boat were incredible. As they ate, the couple watched a whale jump out of the water. *Wow*, Paulina thought, *in all my years I can't believe I've never experienced this*. She thought about how lucky she was to have found Juan and looked up at him, smiling. She leaned over and kissed Brian to show him how much she appreciated the date.

The following morning, Paulina and Brian packed up their belongings and decided to hit the road again to get as far away from Tijuana as possible. There was still no set destination. As they drove, Brian wondered if he had ever taken a road trip with his unknown family.

Brian reclined his car seat. "I wonder if I will ever see my family again. A part of me wants to know who I am, and a part of me is scared about what I may find."

"What scares you the most?"

"The unknown. I mean I could have a wonderful family and awesome friends who were once a part of my life. But then, there's a chance the opposite is true. I feel safe being here with you."

"I love my family so much, and I can't imagine what it would be like to not know them. At the same time, not remembering them makes it impossible to miss them."

"Yeah, that's my problem. I don't miss anyone."

Paulina's forehead creased with concern. "Well, if you ever decide you want to know more about your past, we can save up some money to hire a private investigator after we have jobs."

"Yeah, but I'm starting to feel happy with where I am right now. I don't know if I need anyone else in my life." A smile warmed Brian's lips. "You made everything better for me."

After arriving in a small town outside of Cancun, Brian and Paulina found a cozy two-bedroom home to rent. Brian secured a job as a housekeeper at a motel. He spent his free time practicing Spanish and writing down any random memories that seemed to pop into his head. Paulina began working as a nurse for a family doctor and was happy to be able to remain in the field that she so dearly loved.

Five months later, Brian and Paulina went to the beach for an evening stroll. This is breathtaking." Paulina exhaled. Brian watched as she took in the view.

"Yes, it sure is." He turned toward Paulina and took her hands in his. Paulina glanced over at Brian as he knelt, and she gasped. "Paulina, mi amore, I've loved you since the day we met. I know the stress you've been under is more than anyone should handle, but I know one thing is certain. You've been the only constant in my life as long as

I can remember." He chuckled. "If you would be my wife, it would make me the happiest man in the world." Brian looked deep into Paulina's eyes, as a smile crept across her delicate face.

"Si, mi amor, yes, I will marry you!" She pulled Brian up, and they shared a kiss. Brian picked up Paulina and spun her around.

They found an officiant the next morning and were married on the beach the following week. The wedding's beachfront location was beautiful. Brian and Paulina exchanged vows overlooking the ocean. As Brian and Paulina said, "I do," the sky turned an incredible gradient of pinks, purples, and oranges as the sun started its descent over the horizon. For that single moment, the stresses of the outside world did not matter.

One crisp, spring morning, Brian and Paulina headed into town to do some shopping. They went out together once a month as Brian was still very wary about making his presence known just in case someone was still looking for him. He didn't care if it was Marco's henchmen or his family, at that point it didn't matter anyway. He had a wife, and they had been talking about possibly having a child. This was his life now. Occasionally, Brian found himself still wondering who he was, and if what the men who kidnapped him had said was true. No matter how many times he wondered, he couldn't bring himself to search. *It would be easy enough*, he told himself. Regardless of how easily he could find out, he knew on some level he was better off not knowing. At least for the moment. Brian was happy in his new life and desperately wanted things to work out for himself and Paulina.

One day, Paulina received a box in the mail from her family containing some of her belongings and a newspaper. She pulled out the newspaper and held it up. In bold lettering stood the headline: *John Doe Found Dead*. There was no picture to accompany the story. Paulina showed the article to Brian, and the couple breathed a sigh of relief. They knew, for the moment at least, that they could finally relax. Little did they know, someone was still out looking for him.

TWENTY

Although Kira allowed Ryan to sleep in the guest room, she did not speak to him, and he stayed out of her way. During the week, Ryan escorted Jessica to the school bus and went to work. Although Kira was happy that Jessica had a father in her life, she wanted nothing to do with him. Weeks passed. One day, Ryan received a phone call from Amanda. He still used Brian's cell phone as his own, and she still had no idea who he really was. Ryan felt a pang of guilt as he answered the call.

"Hi, Brian, I have some great news."

"Really? I can certainly use some great news."

"Well, Detective Grimes called me this morning. He thinks they may have found Ryan. There was a news report in Mexico about an unidentified man who lost his memory. He matched Ryan's description."

"That's great! I'm going to book a flight and head there right away. Did he say where in Mexico?"

"He said Tijuana, but don't go there just yet. Maybe wait a couple of days. They want to verify some information. I think they want to make sure it's not some type of scam or mistake. Detective Grimes has a friend who's from there. He's going to have him look into some things first. I'm so excited!"

"My God! That's so wonderful," Ryan exclaimed. "I'm going to book a flight for two days from now. Are you going there too?"

"Actually, I'm in Australia for work. I just had to stay away from that house. If it is Ryan, they might make arrangements for him to fly home, so make sure you check with the detective before you go. I would hate for you to end up in Mexico while your brother is on a flight heading home."

"Duly noted. Is Olivia with you?"

"She's with my parents. I'll be back in a week."

"Well, you just made my day. I finally feel like I can breathe again! I can't wait to tell Kira."

Kira entered into the kitchen as Ryan said her name. "What did you want to tell me?"

"Amanda just told me they might have found Ryan. Hey, Amanda, let's talk later. Keep me updated if you hear any more news."

"Will do. You take care," Amanda said.

Ryan hung up the cell phone. "It feels great to finally get some good news."

"So, where is he?"

"They think he's a John Doe in Mexico who lost his memory."

Kira looked puzzled. "How in the world would he end up in Mexico?"

"I don't know, but that's not important right now. This is so wonderful!" Ryan walked over to Kira and hugged her tightly. "I'm going to go look at flights to Mexico." Ryan left the room and walked over to his computer to research flight information.

Two days later, Ryan was busy packing his bags for his trip to Mexico when the doorbell rang. Ryan glanced at his watch and walked to the front door. When he opened the door, he saw Detective Grimes standing there.

"Hello, Detective. I'm just getting ready to leave for my flight to Mexico."

Detective Grimes had a grim look on his face. "May I come in?"

"Sure." Ryan looked at the detective and noticed that he looked solemn. "Is something wrong?"

"Well, it's about your brother. I really don't know how to say this, but your brother was killed."

"What do you mean? You just found him and said he

was alive," Ryan exclaimed.

"I know. After we were able to confirm that we found your brother, he was killed in a fire. I'm so sorry."

"But...but are you sure it was him? I don't understand."

"I don't have all the details yet, but there was a news report about your brother being killed in a house fire. When we heard what happened, we contacted the police where the fire occurred, and they confirmed everything. The body they found was torched, but they are one hundred percent positive it was your brother. I'm so sorry. I wish I had better news for you."

Ryan fell to his knees and let out a loud yell. Kira ran into the room.

"What's wrong?" Kira said as she glanced down at Ryan balled up on the floor crying. She looked up and saw the detective standing there.

"I'm sorry. Your brother-in-law was killed."

"Oh no!" Kira collapsed onto the floor next to Ryan and wrapped her arms around him. The detective slowly turned and left. Ryan's eyes filled with tears as he tried to look at Kira through blurry eyes. He leaned forward and placed his head on Kira's shoulder.

"It should've been me," Ryan said.

"Don't say that. Neither of you deserved that." Kira tried to find her strength and hold back tears, but suddenly a warm tear dripped from her eye and slowly ran down her cheek. "Did he say what happened?" Kira asked as she lifted the bottom of her blouse and wiped the tears away.

"Something about a fire."

"This just seems so surreal." Kira hopped up and left the room for a few minutes before returning with a box of tissues. After wiping her eyes, she gently dabbed Ryan's face.

"I prayed for information and closure for a long time. I thought no matter what, I would feel better knowing what happened," Ryan said as he grabbed a tissue and blew his nose. "But I don't feel better. There's no more wondering about what happened or where he is, and I don't feel better."

"It'll take time, and we still don't really know what happened to him."

"I remember when someone stole his bike. He was so upset, but then he believed me when I told him my bike was the one that had been stolen. I just let him have that old bike, and he was so happy."

"How did you know which bike was gone?"

"We each had a different sticker on our bike. I told him that I could tell that the bike was his and that the thief must have switched the stickers."

"He actually believed that?"

Ryan chuckled. "I guess he really wanted it to be true."

"Hey, why don't we have a drink? Let's toast to Brian. His favorite wine?" Kira jumped up and poured two glasses of wine. Then, they sat at the kitchen table and spent hours drinking and sharing memories about Brian.

"This wine is really starting to get to me. I guess I'm not used to drinking much."

"I can't believe we finished almost two whole bottles," Ryan said as he shook the second wine bottle.

Kira folded her arms on the table and laid her head on them. "I don't think I'll be able to make it up to bed."

"I got you." Ryan stood and walked over to Kira. "Come on, I'll carry you."

"What?"

"I'll carry you upstairs. Stand up."

"I don't want you dropping me."

"I won't drop you. I'm strong. Stand up." Ryan helped Kira stand and picked her up into his arms, stumbling slightly. "See. I can hold you."

"You better not drop me, or you'll be sleeping in the doghouse," Kira said, slurring her words.

"We don't have a doghouse. I won't drop you." With wobbly legs, Ryan carried Kira up the stairs, almost dropping her twice before throwing her onto the bed.

Kira woke up the next morning to find Ryan in bed next to her. Her head was pounding, and she couldn't remember what happened after he carried her upstairs. She grabbed a pillow, whacked him with it, and attempted to push him out of the bed.

"Ow." Ryan turned and blankly looked at Kira. "Oh, my head."

"Get out!" Kira struck him again. "What are you doing? Get out!" Kira continued hitting Ryan with the pillow until he hopped out of bed and rushed down the stairs.

One week later, Amanda arranged a memorial service for Ryan at a local funeral home. After the service, Kira hosted a repast at her home. When Amanda and Olivia arrived, Kira approached them and hugged Amanda.

"Amanda, if there's anything you need, just let me and Brian know. If you need a babysitter for Olivia or even just a shoulder to cry on, we are here for you." Suddenly, Kira felt weird. She realized that she had just referred to Ryan as Brian without a second thought, even though she knew the truth. Looking at Amanda with tears streaming down her cheeks, Kira wondered what would happen if Amanda knew the truth.

"Thank you for everything, Kira. I don't need anything, but I will keep your offer in mind." Amanda saw Ryan sitting on the sofa in the family room and walked over and sat down next to him. "Brian, I want you to come to my house and pick up any of Ryan's belongings you want. Take as much as you can, okay?"

"I don't want to even think about that. I can't believe he's gone."

"Me either, but I need to get rid of that house. I can barely stand to even look at it. I want to sell it as soon as possible. Please just do me a favor and move whatever you want out of there. I'm hiring a company to do an estate sale."

Ryan sighed. "When's the sale?"

"Hopefully, in about a month, but they're going to go in and inventory everything. You'll need to get what you want before they do the inventory."

"Is it okay if I go there next week?"

"Sure, just let me know when you've picked up everything you want. I hope to have the inventory completed in two or three weeks." Amanda tilted her head and leaned slightly on Ryan's shoulder. "I miss him so much." Amanda sat upright and wiped tears that started rolling down her face with tissue. "I'm sorry. I didn't mean to intrude on your personal space."

"No worries. I never thought I could live without my brother, but I'm doing okay, and you will do okay. They say every day gets better. Hopefully, that's true. By the way, where are you moving?"

"Oh, um, I haven't chosen a permanent home yet. I'm going to Europe for three months, and I plan to have a realtor look for something while I'm gone."

"Are you taking Olivia to Europe also?"

"Well, yeah. Don't worry, I'll make sure she gets to see her favorite uncle. We'll just be gone for a few months. I may start looking for a new job that doesn't require as much travel."

"Well, Kira and I will look after Olivia if you ever need us to. I really don't see you giving up the traveling gig."

"It's starting to not seem as great. Oh, who am I kidding? You're probably right." Amanda dabbed the corners of her eyes with the tissue and walked away to get something to eat.

At the end of the evening, the guests left, and Ryan helped Kira clean up. As Kira carried the punch bowl to the kitchen, Ryan approached her.

"Let me get that for you."

Kira handed Ryan the punch bowl and hurried away. After placing the bowl in the sink, Ryan walked over to Kira.

"I'm sorry. I really mean it. I would change things in a heartbeat if I could."

Kira ignored Ryan and continued cleaning the kitchen table.

"Can we at least talk? You don't have to like me, but

can we at least have a conversation? After last week, I thought there was a chance..."

"A chance for what? Exactly what is there a chance of?" Kira huffed. "Is there a chance I will get my husband back? Is there? Can you do that for me?" Kira stormed out of the kitchen.

Ryan followed Kira. "I can be everything you want. I can be Brian. I am Brian."

"You're insane."

"I'm glad we're finally talking. We always had a special connection. I'm still not sure how Brian ended up with you instead of me."

"Unbelievable!"

"Everyone sees me as Brian. That's who I am now."

Kira glanced at Ryan. *He really does look like Brian. It feels as if he is Brian. Now I'm starting to have crazy thoughts.* "You're not Brian."

"Hey, remember prom? When I was looking for pictures for the memorial, I came across our prom photos. We had such a great time."

Kira sighed. "Yeah, I remember."

"Let's try. We can go on a date. My mom can watch Jessica. Give it a couple of tries, and if things don't work out, I will move out for good, and you won't have to worry about me bothering you anymore."

"I just need time to think."

Ryan grinned. "Take all the time you need."

During the next several weeks, Kira found herself talking to Ryan more with each passing day. Sometimes, she forgot that he wasn't Brian. She saw him as a man who had lost his brother and as her husband. It was easy to do because the brothers looked and acted so much alike. Finally, after three months, she agreed to go on a date with him. Their chemistry was intense, and Kira had a great time on the date. When the evening ended, Kira made a list of the pros and cons of continuing a relationship with Ryan.

Pros: Jessica would have a father. There is greater financial stability. The relationship with him is normally great. Everyone else already believes he is Brian. If people discover the truth, the family's life may be at risk.
Cons: Olivia is left without a father, and Amanda is left without a husband. Staying with Ryan would be living a lie. If he can lie about who he is, can he ever be trusted?

After reviewing the pros and cons, Kira ultimately decided to give Ryan a chance. Before the end of the year, they lived as husband and wife, and Kira maintained Ryan's secret.

Twenty-One

TEN YEARS LATER

Many things changed for the Wrights over the next ten years. After two years passed, Amanda moved into a high-rise condominium and decreased her travel days by 50 percent. Six years later, Amanda married an attorney who worked at her law firm while Olivia attended a local boarding school and was preparing to enter high school. Olivia barely remembered living with her father. She spent most of her summer months and holidays with Ryan and Kira due to her mother's work schedule. She loved spending summers with them, and they developed a close bond.

Ryan still lived his life as Brian, and Kira maintained his secret. They had a second child—a son named Rian who was seven years old. Jessica was a straight A high school student, head cheerleader, and a track star.

It was Saturday afternoon. Ryan and Kira prepared dinner together and sat down to eat with Rian and Jessica.

"I was thinking it might be good to take a trip somewhere for spring break. What does everyone think?" Kira said after she gulped some water.

"I'm down with that. Can I invite a couple of friends?" Jessica said as she pulled out her cell phone.

"I'll think about that. No phones at the table." Kira turned toward Ryan. "Do you think you can take some time off work for a vacation?"

"I'm the boss, so that won't be a problem. Where were you thinking about going?"

"Ooh, let's go to Mexico. Tonya went there last summer, and she said it was really great," Jessica said.

"Which part of Mexico?"

"I'm not sure. I think it was Cancun. Or maybe it was Aruba. I'll ask. Maybe we can stay where she stayed. She said it was luxurious. It was on a large beach, and there were a lot of things to do." Jessica grabbed her cell phone and pulled it out of her pocket again.

Ryan gave Jessica a stern look. "Cell phone down. When is spring break?"

Kira stood up and grabbed her cell phone off the counter. "Let me check the calendar." Kira perused the calendar on her cell phone. "It starts in five weeks. If we decide to go, we'll need to book a resort soon. I'm sure a lot of places are already booked up."

"That works for me. I desperately need a vacation," Ryan said.

Jessica's face lit up with a huge smile. "Can I invite some friends?"

"You can invite two friends, but I need to speak with their parents first. What about you, Rian? Are you ready for a vacation?"

"Yeah!" Rian ran over to Kira. "Can we go swimming?"

"Sure. We can go swimming and snorkeling, and we can build some sandcastles on the beach. Does that sound like fun?"

"Yeah."

Kira walked over to the counter and picked up her laptop. "I will research some resorts. Also, Jessica, check with your friend to see where she stayed. I will look into that place also. I want to have everything booked by the end of the weekend."

Five weeks later, Kira, Ryan, and their kids boarded a plane to Mexico. Two of Jessica's friends were with them. After arriving in Mexico, they took a private shuttle to the resort. Upon arriving at the resort, they checked into a large two-bedroom suite. Jessica and her friends dropped off their luggage in the suite and left to tour the resort and beach. Rian sat down and played his video game while Kira and Ryan spent ten minutes touring the suite and its balcony.

"It is so beautiful here. I can't wait to hit the pool," Kira said as she stepped out onto the balcony.

"Me too. Rian, do you want to go swimming? Go put on your swim trunks."

Rian started searching through his suitcase. Ryan walked over to Rian. "Wait, I'll find them for you." Ryan kneeled on the floor and searched through Rian's suitcase. Finally, he located Rian's swim trunks and handed them to him. Then he grabbed his own swim trunks out of his suitcase.

Kira grabbed her suitcase and rolled it into the bedroom, where she changed into a bikini and cover-up. After the three of them had changed into their swimwear, they left the suite and walked to the resort's infinity pool. They swam, floated, and splashed in the pool for thirty minutes.

Kira swam up to Ryan and Rian. "Hey, are you guys ready to grab a bite to eat?"

Ryan and Rian simultaneously said, "yeah." The three of them got out of the pool and dried off with their towels.

As they walked on the path toward the resort's restaurant, Jessica and her friends ran up to them giggling hysterically.

Kira smiled. "Hey, girls, what's so funny?"

"Oh my God! You will never believe what happened." Jessica laughed so hard she almost toppled over.

"What? What happened?" Kira reached her arms toward Jessica in case she fell over.

"I saw someone who looked like Dad. He was walking across the lobby. I kept yelling 'Dad,' but he didn't turn around. Finally, I ran up to him and tapped him on the shoulder." Jessica giggled. "He turned around and said, 'How may I help you, ma'am?'" Jessica continued laughing.

Kira and Ryan looked at each other. "Jessica, why did you think that was your father?" Kira asked.

"He looked just like Dad."

"Except his hair was different, and he was wearing a suit," Jessica's friend Tonya exclaimed.

"Well, he probably thinks I'm crazy because I just turned around and ran away."

Kira pivoted toward Ryan. "Wouldn't it be weird if that was your brother? After all these years? I mean, what are the odds?"

Ryan stared with a blank look on his face. "Not possible. He's gone."

"His body was burned beyond recognition. How do

we really know that was him?"

"Yeah, maybe Uncle Ryan didn't die in a fire. We should go find that man." Jessica and her friends turned and started walking away.

"Wait, girls. We're going to get something to eat. Why don't you come with us?"

"Don't you want to see if that's your brother?" Jessica said.

"Everyone knows he was killed in a fire ten years ago. Besides, the restaurant is near the lobby. Maybe we'll run into the man you saw on our way to the restaurant, and I'll prove it's not him."

"Okay." Jessica looked disappointed, but she slowly edged closer to her parents.

Everyone headed to the restaurant. After dinner, they wandered around the resort looking to see if there were any signs of the man Jessica saw earlier. After an hour, they returned to their suite and went to bed.

Kira and Ryan woke up early the next morning.

Kira poked Ryan. "Hey, what would you do if that was your brother Jessica saw?"

Ryan sighed. "I really don't know. I would really love to see him, but do you really think he could be alive? Detective Grimes told us he was killed in a fire. I still have a copy of the news article."

"Maybe he was mistaken. The man killed in the fire

was badly burned. They probably really couldn't identify him. He may have just resembled your brother," Kira said.

"I don't know. I really don't believe that was him. You know, they say everyone has a doppelganger. Maybe that was someone who just looked like him."

"Let's see if the girls will let Rian hang with them this morning. Then, we can walk around and see if we can find someone who looks like you. It would be strange if that is him. At the very least, you might find your doppelganger." Kira glanced at the bed where Rian slept and whispered, "If it is your brother, you might need to stop using the name Brian."

"It's been ten years, and it's not like I can even think about going back to Amanda. I'm pretty sure her new husband would not like that. It would be weird to think we had a memorial service for someone who's still alive."

"I'm pretty sure Amanda wouldn't even want you back. And technically, we did have a memorial service for someone who is still alive. Remember? The memorial service was for you, Mr. Ryan Wright."

Ryan sighed. "I can't believe it's been ten years. It's been so long."

"I know it's a long shot, but what if that is your brother? I haven't told you this, but sometimes I dream that he's returned. It seems to only happen after I've had a really stressful day."

Ryan stared blankly at Kira. "What does he do when he comes back?"

"He says he missed me, and it's as if he never left."

"I don't even know what to think about that. Are you saying you would go back to him if he returned?"

"He is my husband. That never changed. Besides, what else could happen? Tell him to continue living your life? It might make sense to switch back to your life."

"So, you would go back to him?"

"It's not about going back to anyone. We are still legally married. Well, we were legally married before his de—"

"Why are we even discussing this? It's not like he can come back from the dead," Ryan yelled, interrupting Kira. Ryan took a deep breath as Kira stared at him stunned.

"I'm sorry," Ryan said as he hugged Kira. "I know it's not easy. It's normal for you to miss him. Even after ten years, I still miss him every day. There's not a single day I don't think about him. Anyway, I'm somewhat excited to find out who my look-alike is. Let's eat breakfast and then go see if we can find my look-alike walking around. We'll let Rian hang with his big sister and her friends while we go on our search mission."

After breakfast, Kira and Ryan left the suite to explore the resort. They stopped by the gift shop to buy snacks. A young woman approached Ryan from behind.

"Juan, I didn't expect to see you on your day off."

Ryan turned around to face the young woman.

"Oh, I'm so sorry. I thought you were the resort manager, Juan," the young woman said.

"Would it be possible for us to speak with Juan?" Kira inquired.

"Oh, is there a problem with your room? Juan is not in today, but I can get the assistant manager for you."

"No, there's no problem with the room. The room is beautiful. Everything is wonderful. We just need to speak with Juan about a personal matter."

Kira turned to look at Ryan, hoping he could come up with a good explanation as to why they wanted to speak with Juan.

"I think he might be a relative I haven't seen in a long time. That's why we look alike."

"Ah, yes. I see. He will be here tomorrow."

Ryan pulled out his business card. "Can you give my card to him and ask him to call me? My cell phone number is on the card. If you want, I can also write my room number on it."

"Just the card will be fine. I will leave the card in his mail slot with a note requesting him to call you."

"Thank you so much."

Kira and Ryan strolled to the beach and dipped their toes into the ocean before returning to their suite. Two days later, Ryan received a call on his cell phone from an unknown number. He held the phone in his hand briefly before answering.

"Hello."

"Hello, this is Juan. You wanted to speak to me?"

"Uh, yes. Can we meet?"

"May I ask what this is regarding?"

"Yeah, um…" Ryan lowered the phone as he pondered what to say next. "Um, I believe you look like someone I know. Does the name Ryan Wright sound familiar to you?"

"No, I don't know that name."

"What about the name Brian Wright? Does that sound familiar?"

Brian paused before responding, "I don't know if I can help you."

"Please, can we meet?"

Brian slid his phone closer as he prepared to hang it up. "I'm sorry, I don't know if I can help. I lost most of my memory a long time ago."

"Well, maybe I can help you. Can we meet? It can be in a public place if you'll be more comfortable with that."

Brian sighed. "Okay, yes. Let's meet in the lobby. Is a half hour good?"

"Yes, that's perfect!" Ryan hung up his phone and turned toward Kira, who was getting dressed. "That was the man who might be my brother. He agreed to meet in a half hour."

"Do you want me to go with you?"

"No, I think it's better if I go alone. I don't want to overwhelm him."

For the last ten years, Ryan traveled with two passports. One contained the name Ryan Wright while the other contained the name Brian Wright. Since Ryan used the name Brian, he always presented the Brian Wright passport when he traveled. However, he held onto the expired Ryan Wright passport as a token to his past life. Ryan stuffed the Ryan Wright passport into his pant pocket and walked to the hotel lobby.

Upon arriving at the hotel lobby, Ryan looked around. There were only a few other people walking through the lobby, and no one was checking in to the resort. Ryan was fifteen minutes early for the meeting, so he sat down on a nearby sofa and perused information on his cell phone. Ten minutes later, Ryan looked up from his phone and noticed a man trudging through the lobby with a security guard near the reception desk. He immediately recognized the man's walk and stood up. As soon as Ryan stood up, the man looked in Ryan's direction and walked toward him with a resort security guard following closely behind.

"Oh, wow. You look just like me." Brian started shaking nervously.

"I'm your twin brother."

"Come, let's go to my office to talk privately." Brian turned toward the security guard. "It's okay. You can leave."

Ryan followed Brian to his office. As the two men walked past the front desk, two workers behind the desk started whispering to each other as they stared at Ryan and Brian walking past them. Once they entered Brian's office, Brian shut the door.

"Please have a seat," Brian said, pointing to the chair in front of his desk. After Ryan sat down, Brian sat down behind his desk. Ryan's eyes scanned Brian's office. In many ways, it was remarkably like Brian's office when he had worked at the dealership. The office colors were the same, and the desk and computer were organized in the same way.

Brian leaned back in his chair and smiled. "I can't believe this. I knew I had to have family somewhere, but I never expected a twin."

"We're identical too. We were told you had been killed in a fire. A detective gave us a copy of two news reports. One was about you losing your memory, and the other was one about you being killed in a fire. He said that your body was burned beyond recognition."

"Ah, yes. My wife arranged for the fake news article because we had no idea if people were still coming after me. We felt it was safer to completely start over, and I really had no idea what was in my past life that would cause someone to harm me," Brian said.

"Do you remember anything about your past life?"

"Most of what I remember is from the past ten years. Occasionally, certain images will flash into my head. I believe they are from my past life, but I don't know who or what they are."

"The news article said that you lost your memory after being shot," Ryan asked.

"Yes, and that's all I really know. I don't even remember being shot. Do you know anything about that?"

"We suspected you might have been shot because there was a bullet hole in your car and a puddle of blood near your car door, but we had no idea why it happened. How did you end up in Mexico?"

Brian shrugged his shoulders. "I have no idea how I got here, but some kids found me in a dump, so the police believe someone shot me and left me for dead."

"So, what have you done during the last decade?"

"Well, I worked my way up to manager of this resort. I started out in housekeeping. I just celebrated my tenth wedding anniversary with my beautiful wife, Paulina. I have a four-year-old son, Pedro. And that's my life in a nutshell."

"So, you're happy?"

"Yes, I guess you can say I'm happy. I do wish I remembered my past life. Was I happy in my past life?"

"Yes, I believe you were happy. You were highly successful, and we were extremely close. We even worked together."

"Your face has a certain familiarity, but I don't know if that's because we look alike." Brian chuckled. "It's starting to make sense now."

"What?"

"Well, I had several dreams where I was with someone who looked like me. I thought maybe it was some weird sign about who I was, but I was dreaming about you the entire time."

"Hey, I have something for you." Ryan pulled the Ryan Wright passport out of his pocket and slid it across the desk to Brian.

Brian looked at the passport and smiled. "Ryan Wright. So, my name is Ryan? That's a nice name. I like it."

"If you ever want to travel, I'm sure you can renew the passport."

"Thank you! Wow, I actually have something from my past life! This is great. I can't wait to tell my family. Well, I mean the rest of my family—Paulina and Pedro. Um, do you mind if I ask you a question?"

"Not at all. Ask any question you want," Ryan said.

"Well, what did I do for a living before?"

"You were the best car salesman in the entire state of California."

Brian's eyes widened. "Really?"

"Well, I might be biased. I thought you were the best. You also sometimes managed the dealership. Since we worked together, we would take turns doing different jobs. Sometimes you would be the salesperson, and sometimes you would be the manager."

"I see. Well, I guess that's why I'm so comfortable being manager of this resort."

"Oh, and you have a daughter. Her name is Jess, I mean Olivia. She's so smart and beautiful."

"Does that mean I was married?"

"It does. Um, she's with someone else now, but she's doing well. I'm sorry. It's been a long time, and everyone believed we would never see you again."

Brian nodded. "I understand. I guess you could say I moved on too."

"Did you ever try to find out who you were?"

"Sure, but as they say, life happens." Brian paused. "I even scheduled an appointment with a private investigator. Paulina was pregnant at the time, and I wanted to make sure I could tell our son something about my family history. Then, she had some complications and they had to deliver early, so I missed the appointment. It was always in the plans for tomorrow."

After meeting with his brother, Ryan returned to the hotel suite, where Kira was anxiously awaiting his return. He didn't know how Kira would react to finding out that Brian was still alive. With every step toward the suite, he wondered what he should say to her. Should he tell her the truth? As soon as he opened the door, Kira hopped up.

"Did you see him? Your look-alike? Who was it?"

"I don't even see why they thought he looked like me."

Kira was shocked, but oddly she felt relieved. "Really? It wasn't Brian?" Kira wrapped her arms around Ryan. "So, tell me, who was your doppelganger?"

Ryan grinned. "I'm kidding. It was my brother."

Kira grabbed a hand towel and slapped Ryan with it. "Stop playin'!"

"I'm serious. It was him. It was Brian. He lost his memory after being attacked, and he's been living in Mexico this whole time."

"You're kidding, right? I don't believe it. Who was it really?"

"Look at me. Look into my eyes. I'm dead serious. He really was Brian."

"Take me to him. I want to see for myself."

"Honey, let's wait. I don't want to overwhelm him right now."

Twenty-Two

It had been eighteen months since Kira and Ryan vacationed in Mexico. They were relaxing at home watching a movie with the kids. Suddenly, the doorbell rang.

Kira picked up her cell phone to check the doorbell camera. "Are you expecting someone?"

"No," Ryan said as he stood up. "I'll go see who's there." Ryan walked to the front door.

"Jessica, did you invite someone over?" Kira asked.

"Ah, ah," Jessica said absentmindedly as she perused web sites on her mobile phone.

"What?"

"I didn't invite anyone," Jessica said without looking up.

As Ryan walked to the front door, he pulled out his

cell phone and looked at the app for the doorbell camera to see who was at the door. As soon as he looked at the app, he stuck the phone back into his pocket and rushed to the front door. Ryan yanked open the door and saw Brian standing there.

"Wow, I didn't expect to see you! Come on in." Ryan hugged Brian squeezing him tightly.

"I hope this is okay. I just received my new passport, and I made a last-minute decision to visit. If you're busy, I can come back tomorrow or whenever you're free."

"Man, don't be ridiculous. You're welcome here anytime. Get in here!" Ryan hugged Brian tightly. "I still miss you every day. Come on back to the family room. We were watching a movie." Brian followed Ryan to the family room. "Hey, everyone, look who's here."

Kira, Jessica, and Rian looked up as Brian entered the room. Kira stood and nervously rubbed her hands down her pants. She walked over to Brian. "Hi, how are you? Jessica and Rian, say hello to your uncle."

Jessica and Rian simultaneously said, "Hi."

"Wow, this is quite a surprise. Come, have a seat," Kira said as she pointed to the couch. She tried hard not to stare at Brian. He seemed so different than she remembered. Physically, he had gained weight, but there was something else. He carried himself differently, and even his speech was different. Every time Kira caught herself staring, she quickly turned away from him.

"Hello, everyone. I don't mean to intrude," Brian said as he sat down on the couch.

"You're family; you're not intruding. Jessica, pause the movie."

Jessica rolled her eyes as she pressed the pause button on the television remote. "May I be excused?"

"No, spend some time with your family." Kira turned toward Brian. "How long are you in town?"

"Just for the weekend." As Brian looked at Kira, he suddenly had what felt like a memory of him kissing her. He glanced up as Ryan walked toward him.

Ryan plopped down onto the couch. "Well, I hope you'll have time to visit Mom. I can drive you to her house tomorrow if you want."

"Sure, that would be great. In fact, that will help me with why I'm here. Since I never fully regained my memory, I would like to learn more about my life before I lost it. During the last ten years, I had random, fleeting images of what I believed to be memories, but they didn't fully make sense. I was hoping to gain insight by coming here."

"We can definitely help. I know there are some old photo albums around here."

"I know where they are. I'll go get them." Ryan stood up and left the room to retrieve the photo albums.

"You don't look like Dad's twin." Rian stared at Brian.

Jessica rolled her eyes. "Twins don't always look alike."

"Twins at my school look alike." Rian picked up a couple of popcorn kernels and threw them at Jessica.

Jessica threw the kernels back at Rian. "Quit throwing stuff. You're too young. You don't understand."

"Actually, your father and your uncle are identical twins. They look a little different now, but they used to look just alike. No one could ever tell them apart," Kira explained.

Rian's eyes widened as he stared at Brian. "Why do you look different now?"

"Rian! Don't be rude." Kira rushed over to Rian and put her hand over his mouth.

"Oh, that's okay. I guess I ate too much of that delicious Mexican food, so now I'm nice and fluffy. Maybe I'll go on a diet so I can look like your dad again."

Rian giggled. "Do you have kids?"

"Yes, I have a five-year-old son. His name is Pedro."

"What about your daughter, Olivia?" Jessica inquired as she stuffed a handful of popcorn into her mouth.

"Who?"

"Your daughter, Olivia. She's thirteen. Here's her picture." Jessica handed Brian her cell phone with a picture of Olivia on the screen. "We don't see her much because she's in boarding school."

"I can't believe I have a daughter I don't even remember. The name Olivia sounds familiar, but I don't remember anything about her." Brian stared at Olivia's photo as tears streamed out of his eyes. "That's what's so hard about what happened. I know there are some people and things I once loved, but I have no memory of them." Brian handed Jessica's phone back to her.

Jessica reviewed some other photos on her phone. "Do you ever think you will have your memory back?"

"I don't know, but looking at photos and learning about the past helps."

"Do you want to move back to America?"

"I don't know. Maybe one day I will move back. I haven't thought about it, but that may be something I'll discuss with my wife one day. I think she might like living here."

Ryan returned with two large photo albums and sat next to Brian. "Are you ready to see some old photos?" Ryan handed one album to Brian. "This album has many old pictures. All of them are before high school. You can see how much we looked alike back then."

Brian flipped through the album's pages. "This is so enlightening. I'm learning so much. A lot of my memories and the images in my head are beginning to make sense."

"Where are you staying during your visit? We have a guest room. You're welcome to stay here."

"I don't want to impose."

"You're family. You're not imposing at all. It will give us a chance to spend more time with each other."

"Well, I guess I can cancel my hotel reservation."

"Great!"

The next morning after eating breakfast, Ryan drove Brian to their mother's house. As they pulled into the driveway, their mother, Margaret, ran out of the house smiling. Ryan walked up to her and gave her a hug. Then she turned to Brian and hugged him tightly. "Welcome home, honey! Welcome home! Come on, let's go in the house." Their mother led them into the home, and the trio walked into the living room and sat down on the sofa. There was a moment of silence. Their mother smiled. "I can't believe it. I can actually tell y'all apart now." Brian and Ryan chuckled.

"Well, don't get too comfortable, Mom. We might fool you again one day," Ryan said.

"Brian, you know you are too old for those childish games. Are you taking Ryan to see Olivia?"

"Actually, I didn't have any plans to take him there," Ryan said.

"You take your brother to see his daughter. Her school only allows visitors on the weekend."

Brian smiled. "I'm here to see family, so I think that's a great idea."

"I'm sure she will be very happy to see you."

Ryan sighed. "Okay, Mom, I will take him to see Olivia as soon as we leave here."

After visiting with their mother, Ryan drove to Olivia's boarding school and checked in. Then he took Brian to Olivia's dorm. When Olivia opened the door, she immediately hugged Ryan. "Hey, Uncle Brian. What are you doing here? Are you still coming to my dance recital next week?"

"Oh, you know I wouldn't miss your recital for the world. Look at who I brought with me."

Olivia stared blankly at Brian.

Brian stepped forward. "Hello, Olivia. It's me, your father."

"Oh, hello."

"Um, well, that's a beautiful locket you're wearing, Olivia," Brian said.

"Thank you. My dad gave it to me. It has a picture of my first... Um, it has a picture of you in it." Olivia opened the locket and showed the picture to Brian.

Ryan also glanced at the locket. "Olivia's stepfather is a cool guy. Hey, why don't I take both of you out to lunch?"

"I had a late breakfast, so I'm really not hungry."

Ryan turned toward Brian. "Can you give me a few minutes?"

"Sure." Brian left Olivia's room.

After Brian left, Ryan sat down at a small round table in Olivia's room. "Olivia, have a seat. Talk to me. What's going on?"

"What do you mean, Uncle Brian?"

"I mean aren't you happy to see your father? You act like you don't even care about him."

"I feel guilty about not being happy to see him. I know he's my father, but he's like a stranger. He's been gone for so long, and I barely have any memories of him," Olivia confessed.

"I understand how you feel. He's my brother, and I feel some guilt about moving on with my life while he was gone. Give it some time. Get to know him again."

⁂

Two months later, the entire family met at a nearby resort for a weekend family reunion. The reunion was attended by Amanda and her husband, Matt, Olivia, Ryan, Kira, Jessica, Rian, Brian, Paulina, and Pedro. Kira and Ryan gathered towels and sunscreen as they prepared to meet everyone by the pool.

"Ryan, we have not discussed what happened in a long time."

Ryan was shocked to hear Kira call him by his actual name. He had not used the name Ryan for what seemed like a lifetime. In his mind, he was Brian, and the name Ryan seemed foreign to him. "What do you mean?"

"Well, do you ever plan to tell your brother the truth?"

"I think we need to think about what will benefit everyone the most. I love my brother, but he seems happy with his current life. His memory loss caused him to be a completely different person. What will telling him everything do?"

"Who knows. Maybe it will help some with his memory."

"He can't go back to being Brian, and I don't even think he'd want to."

Kira had a pensive look on her face. She felt guilty for keeping Ryan's secret for so long, but she could not think of a single way telling Brian the truth would benefit him.

Ryan noticed Kira's worried expression. "Maybe I will speak to him privately and tell him about how we often switched places. I will even tell him about how we shared test taking responsibilities and switched homes and cars when we switched places. The only thing I won't say is that he's really Brian and I'm really Ryan. Knowing that information won't help him at this point in his life. More harm than good will come from revealing that information. I also don't see any real benefit of telling Amanda and the kids."

As Kira and Ryan were beginning to leave their hotel room to meet with their family, Kira turned to Ryan and hugged him. "You know what? Don't tell him about the switching. He's already been through a lot, and there's no need to add a layer of guilt onto his feelings. He deserves to continue feeling happy. Let's just go have fun and enjoy spending time with family."

Ryan looked around the room. "Where are the kids?"

"That's a good question. Rian! Jessica!"

Rian dashed out of his bedroom. Kira wrapped her arms around his shoulders. "Babe, where's your sister?"

"She left with Olivia."

"Okay, we're going downstairs now," Kira said.

Kira, Ryan, and Rian headed to the courtyard where their family reunion barbeque was being held. When they arrived, Jessica and Olivia stood by the picnic table talking as they grabbed plates and silverware near the buffet line. Brian sat at a nearby table next to his wife, Paulina, as he talked to Amanda and her husband. The twins' mother, Margaret, limped toward a table balancing two plates of food. Kira and Ryan greeted Brian and Paulina with hugs.

Suddenly, Rian ran up to Kira and yelled, "Ma, what

did you mean when you said he's really Brian?" Everyone turned to look at Rian.

Kira's eyes widened. "Huh?"

Ryan grabbed Rian's arm. "What did I say about getting in grown folks' conversations? Kids hear half a conversation and act like they know something," Ryan said and chuckled.

Kira breathed a sigh of relief as she looked at Ryan. "Yeah, he probably was confused about what we said." Kira looked around the courtyard to make sure everyone heard what she said. "Honey, you know we told you about how your father and his brother used to switch places, but that was a long time ago."

"Okay, Mommy," Rian said before running off.

THE END

About the Author

K. Redd is a Michigan attorney who enjoys spending her free time writing and various forms of dance lessons, including belly dance and pole dance. *Double Play* is her debut novel. To hear about upcoming releases, visit her on Facebook or sign up for her newsletter.

Facebook:

Newsletter Sign Up: